A BLOODY VINTAGE

A Franklin Starr Mystery

A BLOODY VINTAGE

E S LYNE

GALINEAUX

For all the friends and family who kept faith during this book's long gestation, thank you for your patience.

To you doubters — *booya!*

"The truth is never pure and rarely simple."

Oscar Wilde

CHAPTER

1

"Someone has to die," Starr mumbled apparently out of nowhere. He crouched over the small row of vines that bordered a rough patch of grass in front of his stone terrace. In the early morning silence you could clearly hear the snap of metal against wood as the twisted remains of the previous year's growth were tossed into a wheelbarrow.

"What's this? Middle-aged angst?"

Starr looked up at the small, sinuous figure of Anaïs Dugommier, her face in shadow, her head tilted, ironic. The reference to his age did not go unnoticed.

"In order for the rest of us to value life," continued Starr, ignoring the question and returning to his vines.

"That's cheerful."

"It's from Michael Cunningham's novel about Virginia Woolf – Mrs Dalloway – we saw the movie in Bordeaux, remember?"

"That the one with the suicides?"

"Mmm." Starr finally unbent his body like a paperclip and stood to his full six foot three. He shook the old vine clippings from his hair that had just started to grey at the sideburns before stopping to admire his work: a row of blackened stumps each with a single brown tendril, carefully attached to horizontal wires.

"Now that you're done with the bonsai, is there any chance we might have some breakfast?" Anaïs' voice carried in it the soft sands of her Guadeloupe childhood, the Boston of her university years and a bit of high-heeled Paris. Like the woman, the accent was cosmopolitan.

She looked across Starr's walled garden with its estate agent view of vineyards posed in mathematical precision up the limestone hills in every direction. "I am frozen."

Starr put a bony arm round his lover's shoulders and together they ran into the sudden darkness of the old stone house. A baguette in its twist of paper and two *pains au chocolat* rested on the morning's *Sud Ouest* that in turn rested on the kitchen table. To its side was a half-finished crossword in Starr's messy, italic handwriting. He'd never quite abandoned his old job at *The Times*, even six years out.

Anaïs pulled a chair from under the table and nibbled on one of the *chocolatines*, licking stray pastry flakes into her generous mouth with the tip of her tongue. Starr busied himself with the familiar ritual: coffee beans; grinder; boiling kettle; cafetière.

"You want milk I suppose?" Starr did not approve of diluting coffee with milk, even at breakfast.

"Certainly."

"It'll have to be *longue conservation.*"

Anaïs Dugommier looked up at the her American lover through her thick black lashes and smiled her ironic smile. "*Tant pis.*"

"You know I can't come this evening," said Starr, remembering his promise to go to Guy de Bachelet's annual party. It was an event the patrician wine-maker always held in the week before the *En Primeur* tastings and the single local party Starr grudgingly attended.

"So you said. Wine before art, it will never do," she shook her head.

Starr took down the thick card invitation to the *vernissage* at the smart Bordeaux gallery where Anaïs worked. A photo of some black, ragged material draped over a stick scaffold, a giant electrocuted bat, stared accusingly at him.

"I'm no good at those things," he said. "It's all that money and all that space."

"Yeh – it's OK," said Anaïs. "It's like you said that day we first met, remember? White space, white wine, white people."

Starr felt himself warm up. She'd remembered. He was not in most respects what one might call a vain man, but wordplay was his sandbox and he guarded its toys jealously.

Anaïs checked the large watch that emphasised the smallness of her narrow wrist and got up to go. She kissed Starr full on the mouth, leaning into him, before putting two long, dark fingers up to his lips as if to silence him, and then she was gone, a cloud of dust in her black mini.

Starr was standing watching the empty space where the car had been. It was a morning like any morning, and yet. Something far away, deep in his lizard brain, sounded an alarm. He jumped, as, deep in the house, the phone rang.

"Starr."

"Franklin?" a young woman's voice, hesitant, French accent.

"Sylvie?" Starr chanced — he hadn't heard from his goddaughter — his one and only goddaughter — in, what, a decade?

"Yes, yes. I. I am in Saint-Emilion next week for the *En Primeur* tastings, you know, and I just thought that perhaps we could meet for dinner."

Starr was trying to remember the last time he had seen her. She must have been a young teenager, 13, 14, sitting rather serious, at his stone table on the terrace, carefully tasting a wine and by a process of elimination worthy of Sherlock Holmes, bearing down on its identity, its secret identity.

"Sure," he said. "You still working for that wine mag?"

"*Cuvée*, yes. I am impressed that you are remembering."

"I'll book us a table at *Le Tertre*. What's a good evening?"

"Well, I arrive on Tuesday so Wednesday perhaps – is Wednesday OK?"

"Perfect. *Le Tertre*, 8 o'clock."

Starr walked slowly back into the kitchen. Sylvie, Agnès' only child, had been a serious teenager, adult before her time. Why was she getting in touch now? Did she need cash? Starr pondered as he swilled the large handleless cups under the tap.

Later that evening he stood awkwardly in his one suit, the long sleeves of his Brooks Brothers shirt extending beyond the coat's cuffs, already regretting his decision to come.

A large, blowsy woman advanced towards him across the magnificent stone-flagged salon, grasping a glass of Champagne in her pink swollen fingers, each imprisoned in an array of shiny, tight rings.

"Are you a foreigner too? " she barked.

"No, I am American," Starr replied.

"Ah yes well, you're almost one of us," the woman's voice trailed off as Starr waved at an imaginary acquaintance and strode purposefully away.

"You offending people already?" her red-faced husband said as he drew level.

"American."

"Oh heaven preserve us. A septic. Do you think he plays golf?" he added perkily.

The elegant room was filling up; its enormous stone fireplaces were curving parentheses grasping the flock of guests at each end like a witty aside. The floor-to-ceiling French doors that punctuated the length of one wall were flung open to the flagged terrace, the view of the serried ranks of vine stumps stretching into the distance with the precision of a Normandy war cemetery, their gnarled stumps just showing the first signs of green growth – as green, as Colette once said, as a tree frog after a tropical storm.

Starr made it to the tasting bench where a disciplined, almost monastic, line of glasses stood quietly waiting to be blessed by one of the chateau's many award-winning vintages. A tall, balding man in his late sixties, impeccably but quietly dressed, touched his elbow.

"*Monsieur Starr* – I am so glad you could come," he spoke cultured, accented English. "Please, tell me what you think of this. It's our second growth and still a little young but I must confess I am quite excited by it." He nodded imperceptibly to the young flunky behind the bench who, with immense concentration, poured perhaps a tablespoon of wine into a large glass and gave it to Starr.

Starr knew the drill. He'd lived on the edge of the great Saint-Emilion estates for 12 years now, on and off, and since the death of his wife, wine had become his best friend. He swirled the dark red liquid round the edge of the glass watching it cling to the sides before taking a good long sniff.

Guy de Bachelet raised an aristocratic eyebrow in enquiry.

Starr smiled at him. "Second growth you said?"

De Bachelet nodded.

Starr took a decent swig and felt the wine bloom in his mouth. In vino veritas. In wine there is truth, he thought to himself as he swallowed. He wasn't a spitter.

"It might be a bit subtle for Parker," said Starr. "But I can see why you're excited."

De Bachelet looked very directly into Starr's unblinking petrol blue eyes. "My banker will not thank me for saying this, but you know I don't care what *Monsieur Parker* thinks. This is a great wine, by any standards. If he wants to give 90 points to some brash *garagiste* with the finesse of a right hook, that's up to him." His cashmere-clad shoulders rose upwards in the faintest Gallic shrug which, in that one small gesture, managed to convey that he had been making wine all his life, that his family had been tending this estate for over 300 years and most of all that he was far too refined to say so.

"Excuse me, but I have to see these *négociants* and that Chinaman. He is a billionaire three times over, you know, and all from making air conditioning units," the aristocrat stopped just short of sneering, but only just.

Starr spent the next 40 minutes or so, meeting and avoiding in equal measure, the local estate owners, the wine brokers, the billionaire buyers whispering to their wine advisers, the English novelists terrified by the possibility of each other's success and the various members of subtly different social tribes that, like a Venn diagram, overlapped at this gathering.

"Franklin!" the familiar voice, full of the Lancashire moors, called from across the room. "You trying to avoid me?"

"Jim! Thank God."

"Christ, I hate these bloody things."

"I thought this was your natural habitat, Jim. Chateau owners, *négociants*, starry vintages, the cut and thrust of a deal."

"Give me a break. This is hell. Since Chateau Benedictus was promoted to Grand Cru Classé A status, every grubby little broker has been here oiling up to de Bachelet trying to up their allocations."

"Can't see that working, can you?"

In response, Jim Shawcross took a large swig of his red wine, blinked theatrically and pronounced,

"It ain't half bad, though."

Starr smiled. Jim Shawcross was one of the most unlikely features of this hallowed landscape. Starr defied anyone to guess what lay beneath the poorly shaven, dishevelled Lancastrian. He represented one of the two oldest English importers of fine Bordeaux – a company whose cellars apparently stretched from its old shop in London's Mayfair under St James' Palace, across the Mall and down to the river itself. There wasn't anyone who was anyone in the multi-billion euro wine trade who didn't know Jim.

He had an encyclopaedic knowledge of wine: his tasting memory was leviathan. He could determine the finest nuances of anything he tasted, understand, catalogue, compare and recall hundreds, thousands even, of the first and second growths of the great chateaux that stretched along the banks of the two great *mers*: the Garonne and the Dordogne. Starr owed everything he knew about wine, which wasn't much, to this overweight, badly-dressed Englishman.

"I thought the Chinese were only interested in older vintages to drink now. Auctions. Are they buying *en primeur* too?"

"Mmm some are," Jim Shawcross shook his burly head from side to side. "Although this is just the overture – there's no real business until next week."

Starr watched Shawcross scan the room and frown but he couldn't see who or what had unsettled him. With a bluff "I'll catch up with you another time," he was ploughing his bulky frame back through the sea of guests.

He managed to escape onto the terrace for a quick Camel Light. It was the first step to giving up. He would give up, now that he had a girlfriend who didn't smoke. He inhaled deeply. In the summer, when the weather was better. He crossed the terrace in his loping stride to a stone bench and as he sat down his right knee cracked as it had started to do. Two girls, one on each knee, he thought, remembering the great Roger Squires clue. Sadly not his own. Pat. Ella. Patella.

One of the *négociants* he'd clocked earlier was loading a wine crate into the front of his Porsche, lightly tossing it into the small trunk under the hood. Something snagged in Starr's brain, like a cracked nail on a cashmere jersey, but he didn't know why. He recognised, but couldn't place him. He was the wrong side of 40, but not by much; tanned, slim, his longish hair swept back from his forehead. Unmistakably French. The gravel flew as the 911 turned and disappeared up the cedar-lined drive through the chateau gates.

The early spring sun had left the far hillsides and Starr shivered slightly as the temperature dropped like a stone down a well and a bitter wind ruffled the pale tendrils of the new year's vintage. Time to go home.

"Am I late?" Sylvie asked anxiously.

"Not at all – you are perfectly on time," Starr rose to kiss her. He couldn't stop grinning. For all the neglect that he had showered on his only goddaughter, her presence here in front of him made him feel ridiculously happy.

The maître d' hovered, not just doing his job, but clearly curious that the American had landed such a peach of a girl.

Two chilled flutes of Kir Royales arrived at the table, as if by telepathy.

"How's the Petit Girondine – still got those lumpy beds?" Starr clinked glasses.

"Oh you know it?" Sylvie was surprised. "It is very comfortable. Not 'lumpy' at all. Maman was insistent I stay there." She continued, "You look very well."

"Not half as well as you," Starr raised a glass in toast, "It's great to see you."

Starr's mind wandered back to those fleeting weekends he had snatched with Sylvie's mother, Agnès, at the small, provincial hotel. They had never fitted together as he did with Esmé, but in one way they had been closer soulmates. She doing her doctorate at the university in Bordeaux and he on the seven year sabbatical *The Times* used to hand out in those golden years, improving his French. It would never have worked, he sighed into his Champagne.

Le Tertre was the epitome of Starr's idea of what a good restaurant should be. Not large, not over-fussy, with a cuisine that was filled with the flavours of the *terroir*: salty goat's cheese with a Mirabelle chutney; the musty truffles and wild boar of the Perigord Noir; oysters from the great sandy shores of Arcachon; fat prunes and sweet walnuts; and a truly great library, a fine art gallery of wines from this epicentre of viniculture. Here you could still find a '53 Lafite Rothschild or a '61 Haut Brion, kept in perfect conditions, undisturbed in the limestone *cave* at the back of the restaurant in which they sat. Starr had been studying the wine list for a while before he ordered a bottle of '88 Pichon Lalande, silently pointing to it and knowing that the wine would be decanted properly in front of them. It should complement perfectly the steak he had ordered for himself and Sylvie's choice of roasted pheasant with truffle oil.

"I want you to taste this blind," Starr invited.

"OK, sure," Sylvie laughed. "It will be like 12 years ago on your terrace all over again!"

The sommelier poured a few centimetres of the rich red wine into Sylvie's glass. She shook it a little and then twirled it in the glass, admiring its colour in the candle flame. "Lovely inky colour, " she noted, before taking a long deep breath from the top of the glass. "Pencil lead, smokiness and cedar." She was concentrating deeply, lost in the experience of the wine. "Classic Pauillac nose?" the upward inflection of her accented English appealed to Starr.

"Right on the money so far," he encouraged her.

"Mature, inky, quite meaty, quite seductive," Sylvie continued having only now taken a good sip. The sommelier looked on, appreciatively.

"The wine is fully integrated with a perfect balance of tannin and fruit. I think it is from one of the better vintages of the late eighties," she continued.

"Any advance on Pauillac?" pressed Starr.

"Oh didn't I say? It's definitely Pichon. Pichon Lalande…eighty-eight!" The sommelier turned the creamy label bearing the aristocratic gold lettering of the Comtesse de Lalande toward her and poured the wine into her and Starr's glasses.

"That's my goddaughter!" exclaimed Starr. "I never doubted you. Not for one moment."

"Are you still doing your crosswords?" Sylvie asked.

"I try not to. But *The Times* still gets me for Easter and Thanksgiving… and sometimes in between, if they get stuck, for a Friday." Starr replied.

"Friday?" Sylvie rolled her 'r's in proper French fashion.

"Oh yeh. *The New York Times* has a long-standing tradition of increasing the difficulty of crosswords during the week. So Monday is a pretty easy ride but by the time you get to Friday it's supposed to be tough. I like to think that, as we cruciverbalists go, I can still hammer out a fiendishly difficult clue."

"I bet you can," Sylvie laughed. "Full of all those Latin allusions and abstruse chemical formulae."

"It's true I'm a bit of a lapsed classicist," admitted Starr, "But my science has always been strictly schoolroom. That bastard, Joseph B Klimper – he's the guy for formulae."

"I never forget what you once told me at La Borie," Sylvie seemed serious now. "You said your job was to mean what you say but not necessarily say what you mean. I never forgot that."

"Aha! I was just trying to impress you with some wordplay."

"Do you still use that funny name, err Gark something?"

"Yes, well remembered. Garkbit. He's the methane-breathing waiter in Douglas Adams' restaurant at the end of the world. All crossword compilers have pseudos, you know."

"Perhaps I can persuade Gilles to include a wine crossword in *Cuvée?*"

"Who's Gilles?" Starr asked innocently.

"Gilles," Sylvie coloured involuntarily. "He's my Editor."

"Ah," Starr saw Sylvie's train of thought light up, carriage by carriage. "Your lover too?"

Sylvie cast him a quick, defiant flash of her grey, or were they green, eyes. "Of course not. He is married you know. Very married."

"Famously married too," Starr couldn't help himself. "Isn't his wife the Brie-Bonnard fragrance house heiress?"

"Yes, yes...do you know her?" Sylvie coloured some more.

"Gosh no. Only from the pages of *Hello!* I don't read."

Sylvie lowered her eyes.

"I'd be delighted to compile for *Cuvée*," Starr broke the silence. "Honoured. Put me on your subscription list so I can indulge in some serious wine porn. All those luscious wines, mmm..." Starr licked his lips in a theatrical pose of lascivious longing.

"You remind me of a flirtatious *négociant* I met at the tastings yesterday," continued Sylvie.

"Really?"

"He was very *charmant*, and very flattering but old. Well not old old." Starr knew that he fell into the 'old old' category. "Perhaps in his thirties. Quite good-looking, you know, and very knowledgeable about wine of course."

"Well you'd certainly hope so," laughed Starr.

"He admired my tasting notes and invited me back to his, how you say, office?"

"To admire his etchings?"

"Etchings?" Sylvie was lost.

"Ignore me. I'm playing with you. So did you go to the flirtatious negociant's lair?"

"Well I must admit I did. He had a Porsche *décapotable* err 911– you know – the new Carrera 4S."

"Ah so it was the Porsche, not the wine, that turned your head?"

"Well I'm not sure. Something was a little fascinating about him."

"Does he have a name?"

"Damien Refeuille. Actually he operates here – from Saint-Emilion – in a little room above les Trois Etoiles."

"The bar?" Starr knew the place well. "That's quite unusual not to have his office in Bordeaux, isn't it?"

"I suppose it is. And he has some really extraordinary vintages in his collection. Rare wines – wines that you never see coming up for auction any more. Mostly pre-1972. He sells to private clients in the United States."

"That's not unusual, although the Far East is more on the money now. Perhaps he has family connections with some of the old chateaux-owners. What was his office like?"

"It was very small with just three desks and a little simple tasting bench. He had some wine open for me to taste, but something very odd happened," Sylvie lent forward and lowered her voice, as if what she was about to say was a deep and dark secret.

"It was a Romanée-Conti '45!"

"No! "exclaimed Starr, astonished and disbelieving in equal parts. "But the whole vintage is either drunk or in private hands surely?"

"Exactly what I said. But the wine was no way a Romanée-Conti, let alone a '45. I'd be surprised if it was more than five years old."

"Did you tell this Refeuille what you thought?"

"Yes of course," said Sylvie, "I immediately told him the wine could not possibly be what the label suggested. But he showed me the cork and I examined the bottle. It all looked right – perfect. But the wine said otherwise."

"In vino veritas. What was his response?" asked Starr.

"He was a little flustered initially. I suppose it was very bad news. After all a Romanée-Conti '45 has got to be worth at least €8,000 a bottle, maybe more. But then he was very charming and thanked me and said he was going to ask questions of the chateau, etcetera. He even offered to buy me dinner."

"Did you go?"

"It's Thursday night actually. You should be flattered because he wanted to take me out tonight, but I told him I couldn't change our rendez-vous."

"I'm glad. Be careful Sylvie. These négociants can be a slippery breed you know. It's all about the money for them."

"Oh I know, but he wants to investigate too. It will make a great story for *Cuvée*, and Damien has offered to help me research the background."

Starr ordered them each a glass of a fine Marquis de Montesquiou Armagnac '63 and suggested that Sylvie come to stay with her mother some time when she wouldn't be working so hard. "I will definitely," she pressed Starr's hand firmly at the hotel door and then reached up to kiss him chastely on each cheek.

It was a fine, cold night and Starr decided to walk the couple of streets to the Place de l'eglise Monolithe, its famous limestone tower floodlit and icy white against the black velvet sky. Saint-Emilion, with its unspoilt Romanesque churches and towers, surrounded by the great vineyards, was nevertheless a little eerie at night.

By day you could almost smell the money in its immaculate, old streets. How the poor old hermit Emilion would turn in his grave at the Range Rovers, Ferraris and Lambos negotiating the narrow turns and small squares of the ancient little town. But the night belonged to much older spirits: the pilgrims on their way to Santiago de Compostela, the knights Templar, and long, long before them cro-Magnon man whose enigmatic graffiti could still be found in the labyrinthine caves that provided kilometres of interlocking tunnels, like prehistoric metro lines criss-crossing under the limestone escarpment.

Sylvie Janneau was an interesting girl: beautiful without quite knowing it, intelligent and precocious in her knowledge and understanding of wine, but also somehow unsettled, naïve even. She's not quite formed, thought Starr, protectively, and shuddered as the cold night finally penetrated his old wool coat.

The freshly buttered sky shone blue even now at not yet seven in the morning over the undulating fields of vine stumps, stretching like metalwork sculptures in precise rows as far the eye could see. Deep geometry governed the vine armies marching like toy soldiers across the poor soil of the Gironde. It was a still landscape, disturbed only by the smallest swirl of dust that denoted a car moving at speed along one of the chalky white lanes between the vineyards. As it came into earshot, Starr peered up over his glasses from his *Sud-Ouest*, squinting in the early sunlight at the pleasingly dented once-white 2CV van steadily coming into view.

Starr was an early riser. He liked the luxury of being awake as his peers, competitors in the race of life, slept heavily in their beds. It gave him a mysterious advantage, he felt. The van disappeared from view briefly before reappearing on the pale gravel of La Borie's driveway where it jerked to a sudden stop.

Starr struggled in vain to mask his irritation at having his early routine disturbed.

"*Bonjour Monsieur Starr.*" The van driver spoke with the strong "ang" sounds of the local Occidentale accent. He wore thin linen trousers that flapped above the ankle revealing tanned and hairy feet that were encased in dusty sandals made from plaited plastic. His top half sported a multi-patterned thick acrylic jumper which, judging by its general filth, had been glued to his body for the whole of the winter.

"*Bonjour à vous,*" Starr replied non-commitedly.

"*Je suis ici pour les fenêtres,*" explained the man, gesticulating at the admittedly rain-stained windows of Starr's old stone house. Starr's long immersion in rural France had taught him passable French, to know a decent wine from an execrable one, the rules of rugby. But 12 years' of exposure to the culture and people of the Gironde had failed to help him understand the French system when it came to services. You could call twenty window-cleaners and receive assurances that they would come to your house "*tout-de-suite*" or "*à la prochaine*" and put safe money on no-one turning up. But now, and this wasn't the first time it had happened, without any appointment or indeed previous contact, a window-cleaner arrives at 6.45am, as if this was the most natural thing in the world.

The man was busy unloading ladders and pointed dramatically to the bucket. He had clocked that Starr was clearly an imbecile, as are all Americans, and communication thenceforth had to be in exaggerated sign language.

Starr considered interrogating the man, why he was there, who had asked him to come, but soon thought better of it and returned to the terrace. A large trailer-load of seasoned oak logs had been delivered, again without *commande*, the previous October and earlier in the month a *specialiste* had turned up to check his *fosse septique*. It was, when one thought about it, better to accept that life's little essentials would eventually be ministered to, and throw away the *Pages Jaunes*.

Starr refilled his coffee from the cafetière on the table.

"*Café?*" he shouted up to Monsieur Acrylic Jumper. "*Avec plaisir!*" the man shouted down. Starr got a small cup from the kitchen and poured the thick, dark liquid into it.

"*Belle vue*," opined the window cleaner, stretching one arm across the panorama of criss-crossing vines while the other was busy heaving the contents of Starr's sugar bowl into the tiny cup.

Starr muttered something about the complexities of viniculture: the attention to detail, the subtle art of maturation and blending.

"Bah!" humphed M. Acrylic Jumper. "God does all the work," and turned back to his duties on Starr's windows.

Deep in the house behind him, a telephone rang.

"*Téléphone!*" shouted the window-cleaner redundantly from the top of his ladder.

Starr blinked in the sudden darkness of the cold house, "*Oui 'allo, Starr*," he answered.

"*Viens immédiatement, un catastophe.* The ruins of the Dominican convent." The caller hung up. Starr chewed over the possibilities in his mind. Guy de Bachelet was not a man easily ruffled.

Starr shoved his sockless feet into a pair of deck shoes, grabbed a coat from a random selection that hung in the hallway and, mind racing, urged the old Peugeot 607 into spluttering life.

"*Je reste jusquà votre retourne. Pas de problème*," shouted the window-cleaner, Starr temporarily oblivious to his presence at the house.

Soon he was bowling down the chalky lanes that criss-crossed the Saint-Emilion vineyards, slowly climbing up to the limestone escarpment that was home to many of the very grandest *crus* of the region. He hummed the tune to Fats Waller's 'Smashin Thirds'.

The ruined three Gothic arches of the Dominican convent on the outskirts of Saint-Emilion stood like an enormous gatehouse to the town. As Starr approached, he could see a blue gendarme van was parked across the road and more police were unrolling the red and white cordon that circumscribed a crime scene. Closer to the convent ruin, he could see an ambulance and parked next to it de Bachelet's old Mercedes.

Starr scrolled impatiently through his cellphone's contacts folder to find de Bachelet's number. Not under 'D' eventually he found it under 'B.' Reception at La Borie was non-existent but up here on the outskirts of the town he noted the three bar signal with relief.

"De Bachelet?"

"*Oui, Monsieur Starr,*" de Bachelet's voice was taut.

"I am here on the D2. I can see your car, but the police have blocked the road."

"Wait there. I am coming."

The tall, elegant figure of the distinguished vineyard owner came into Starr's line of vision. He was accompanied by one of the gendarmes.

"So young," was all he managed to say.

"What has happened, *Monsieur?*" Starr asked the gendarme.

"I regret that the body of a young woman has been discovered. She is dead. We are in the process of identifying her."

"Starr, I know who she is," blurted out de Bachelet, grabbing Starr's arm. "She is a journalist. Here for the *en primeur* tastings. She left a message at the chateau yesterday. Wanted to interview me for *Cuvée*. The police called me because I was the last number she dialled on her *portable.*" There was a short pause as the aristocrat lifted his eyes to focus on the horizon. "But we never did get to meet," he said slowly. "She never came."

Starr felt the blood leave his face and the many years of inaction, of masterly avoidance and studied langour seemed to leave him with it, like an exorcised ghost.

"I know who she is. I can identify her," he said to the gendarme.

CHAPTER

2

Starr sipped his espresso in the station café, out of the brisk wind that had suddenly whipped up. He was early, of course. The TGV from Paris wouldn't be here for at least 20 minutes, but he liked to be in front, waiting.

He had only seen one dead body in his life: his mother in her nursing home, already arranged by the staff. Pale and lifeless, eyelids closed. This was altogether different. Sylvie's body had been cut down by the time he got there but the blue nylon rope remained around her neck and the livid purple welts had not yet turned brown. Her mouth was open and her tongue protruded. There was dribble down her chin. Her legs were swollen and purplish through her tights. He forced himself to remember every detail, every shocking detail.

The police clearly thought it was suicide, although they couldn't pronounce officially at least until the post-mortem had been completed. But why would Sylvie want to kill herself? And even if she did, why walk to the edge of the town, stand on three old wine crates and hang yourself on one of the iron braces across a ruined arch? It made no sense.

His musings were interrupted by the blast of the station's intercom announcing the imminent arrival of the TGV from Paris.

Most of the people who had got up early enough to make the first TGV to Libourne out of Paris were businessmen, he noted. They all made purposely for the exit while he scanned the long train for signs of Agnès, and then suddenly there she was, chic as ever, with her blonde hair swept back away from her forehead and wearing a light blue tweedy coat. Her face was drawn and tired. Starr didn't suppose she'd slept since the grim news had finally reached her in Cairo the day before. She'd been there on a conference and it was now three days since Sylvie's body had been found.

They drove the six kilometres to La Borie in silence, she looking out of the window over the undulating landscape and he concentrating more than was necessary on the road ahead.

Sitting at La Borie's dented and split raw elm kitchen table, Agnès' wiped her tear-damp face with her sleeve, suddenly looking like a six year old girl, thought Starr.

"I don't know what to say," he said. "I can't believe it was suicide."

"Oh but that's always what the family says," Agnès replied bitterly, "I cannot bear to think how miserable she must have been. How I should have said more. Said what was in my heart."

Starr stopped himself for a moment, but then continued. "She hinted perhaps she had feelings for de Cazaux – her boss," the inflection of his voice rose upward in a tentative question, as he tiptoed toward the subject.

"You mean Gilles, the editor?" Agnès stared straight at him, her violet eyes still beautiful and unchanged by the years. Starr shrugged in affirmation. "Oh no. You have that all wrong. Sylvie was gay. It was Gilles' wife, Marie-Joëlle, that had started to wreck her life."

Starr was for once lost for words. Of course, at *The Times* he had come across a few bright, dedicated, often funny women, who had made it clear that they had no interest in his attentions or those of any man. But Sylvie? How could that possibly be true?

"You can't be serious," he finally resorted to cliché.

"Oh absolutely. She told me on her twelfth birthday. 'Maman, I prefer girls. You had better get used to it.' I must admit at the time I thought it was just part of an intelligent girl's natural rebelliousness, you know. She always had boys interested in her, and I thought best to play it cool and wait for her to find love. But I should have known with Sylvie she meant what she said and it was always girls with her. But that wasn't really a problem – she seemed happy. I sort of got used to it and then she went to work for *Cuvée*. De Cazaux took her under his wing and before long she was invited to their apartment in the 16th, and then the family house in Charly-sur-Marne for weekends."

Starr was listening intently. This opened a whole new set of questions in his mind, but he knew how to be patient with his old friend.

"I encouraged her," Agnès caught her breath, not sobbing, but close to it. "I mean they were such a golden couple. De Cazaux heading up one of Paris' most successful magazines with his famous, aristocratic heiress wife and their faultless twin boys – it just seemed so good for Sylvie. I really thought so," she looked up at Starr for reassurance.

"It was quite natural. Anyway Sylvie would have done what she wanted, with or without your encouragement, I suspect."

Agnès smiled. "Yes, she always drove her own route – is that how you say it?"

"Went her own way," nodded Starr.

"Anyway the first I knew something was going on was on her birthday, you know, last month. She had become a little preoccupied, but I had no idea. Her little flat in the Place Clichy was filled, I mean literally filled, with flowers – I've never seen anything like it. And there was this card from Marie-Joëlle. With this, you know, intimate message. I realised then that Sylvie was in deep – too deep. Out of her depth. Marie-Joëlle was I think playing with her. A much younger woman, attractive, eager – and also I suspect using it to annoy Gilles. To keep him dancing, not too comfortable and secure."

"Poor Sylvie," Starr reached across the table and put his large, tanned hand on Agnès' arm.

"I didn't know what to say," Agnès continued. "Sylvie thought Marie-Joëlle was going to leave Gilles and the boys for her. It was so obviously never going to happen, but if I said so, it seemed I wasn't taking the relationship seriously, and Sylvie was very, very serious about it. I was worried for her though. Did you know the woman took her to Morocco for a long weekend, to some amazing hotel in the desert. She dazzled her. She gave her expensive presents and all the while Sylvie was

going into the editorial offices of *Cuvée*and reporting to her husband."
Agnès looked worn out.

"Let me get you some strong coffee," Starr put the chipped enamel
kettle on the hob and took down a pair of mugs from an old cupboard
above the sink.

The two took the steaming coffee out of the kitchen to the stone
terrace where the vines were only just showing signs of green life but
the spring sunshine was warm.

"You know Franklin," Agnès pronounced his name with attractive
difficulty, "This is such a beautiful house. You were clever to buy it. I
would never have seen its potential."

"No you would have run a mile!" Starr laughed. "It was a pile of
rubble with blown walls, ivy sticking out of the roof and swallows
nesting in the bedrooms. But we bought it for this." Starr turned his two
hands up to the sky and in that small gesture indicated the vast unbroken
view in front of them, of little parcels of vineyard, each with its own
closely guarded character, each subtly different from its neighbour and
each producing a mysterious nectar that had captivated human beings
for thousands of years.

The plural pronoun wasn't lost on Agnès. "Do you miss her terribly?
Esmé?"

"Sometimes," admitted Starr. "But it's a long time ago now. A
different chapter. She'll always be part of me, of my life, but you put
down new layers of memory and although it never goes away, the pain, it
does change subtly. There's a kind of emptiness that replaces the sadness.
You know, you don't just lose the person, but you lose your future with
that person. All the plans, the might-have-beens. The hardest thing is
getting back to feeling involved in life."

Starr thought, fleetingly, that Sylvie's death had been the first time
since Esmé had finally left him, that he felt that sense of purpose, the
will to engage. He wasn't going to take any shit from the police. He could
not believe she had taken her life – she had been too full of it, too full
of the future.

Agnès sighed and leant back against the stone bench running her
hands through her still blonde hair, when a sudden crunch on the gravel

shattered the moment. "If it's not the man from Porlock it's a French peasant," he grimaced and got up to deal with Monsieur Acrylic Jumper.

The window cleaner extracted himself from the beat-up old 2CV van and raised his voice to talk to the imbecilic American, "*La toiture*," he pointed up to the house's uneven covering of Roman titles, like terracotta drainpipes that had been cut in half lengthways. And without further explanation began to free his ladder from the roof and prop it up against the house. Starr returned to Agnès on the terrace with the cafetière as the man, whose name Starr still didn't know, began to replace cracked tiles from a pile he had in the back of his van.

"You know if I were a Greek or Roman, I would be convinced that this man had been sent by one of the gods to mess with my destiny," Starr explained to Agnès. "He turned up, the morning of, um, Sylvie being discovered without warning to clean my windows and now he's back to fix the roof!"

"That's normal for the countryside," Agnès smiled indulgently at Starr's Anglo-Saxon need for logic and order.

Starr had reserved a table at one of his favourite (and there were many) restaurants – La Belvédère. First impressions weren't promising. With the aesthetics of a roadside café, complete with plastic floral tablecloths, a wrap-around sixties terrace and a dark, cramped interior, this *resto gastronomique* was hard to find and stood on its own with an inadequate slope of car park beneath. But initial impressions were, in this case, misleading. The restaurant was sited right on the edge of a high escarpment overlooking the mighty, curling Dordogne river high above the medieval bastide town of Castillon whose twinkling lights drew the eye down into the valley and across to the escarpment on which sat Saint-Emilion beyond. The view was extraordinary, but the food was more so.

As with many fine establishments, La Belvédère was run by a husband-and-wife team: he king of the kitchen and she queen of front of house and the starry wine list. They rowed and bickered incessantly and their volcanic relationship did not spare *les clients*. On the pine-panelled walls of the cabin-like structure were the badges of excellence that La Belvédère richly earned year after year.

Starr had had difficulty persuading Agnès to come along, but he knew that festering in her misery at La Borie was the last thing she needed. Somehow, life must go on.

Madame Chabron kissed Starr warmly on each cheek and welcomed Agnès to the restaurant. "How is he?" asked Starr sotto voce. "*Comme toujours. Il me fait suer, ce sac de viande!*" Madame Chabron's insults were up to scratch, Starr noted and just then the old bag of meat himself appeared. Starr was pressed within the starched folds of Monsieur Chabron's monster embrace and taken, confidentially, to the back of the restaurant into the kitchen. There, on the spotless steel surfaces, were little ramekins of courgette soufflé ready to go into the oven, a veal jus was reducing to syrupy heaven in a copper pan on the huge range and as Chabron opened the massive refrigerator, Starr saw trays of impossibly beautiful dessert concoctions; architectural works of art in jewel colours.

Starr returned to the terrace table and was pleased to see that Madame Chabron was making Agnès laugh with one of her many tales at her husband's expense. "*Il est vachement idiot!*" she exclaimed and cheerfully left them to tend to other clients. "Menu or carte?" asked Agnès over the top of her plastic maroon bound menu, struggling to kill the gloom that theatened to engulf them. Two glasses of Kir Royale with the tiniest little *amuses-bouches* arrived to sustain them during their deliberations.

"Let's go for the Menu Aquitaine" suggested Starr, who knew that the loftiest reaches of Monsieur Chabron's culinary masterpieces were reserved for the most complex, and expensive, menu. He hoped that La Belvédère could succeed where empty words failed in restoring their spirits.

The list of delicacies was a royal feast. There was lobster poached in Champagne; a salad of smoked salmon and noix Saint Jacques, fished out of the Atlantic not an hour up river that morning and then refreshed with a raspberry vinegar. Agnès chose the *velouté d'as*perges (which were just in season) and Starr ignored the *foie gras*, which Anaïs had convinced him could never be eaten once you knew the back-story, and instead opted for a trout pâté. They then agreed to share the legendary *Chateaubriand* *au poivre de Séchouan* that was unmissable, cheese from the region and postpone deciding on dessert from the Carte Gourmande until later. The food organised, Starr turned his mind to the luscious wine list. Not quite on the scale of Le Tertre, it was nevertheless a thing of beauty, with tempting detours and diversions from the best-known chateaux that showed the Chabrons knew their *terroir* and their clientèle.

Starr ordered them both a glass of Clairet (Bordeaux's very particular brand of rosé). Passing by the more obvious clarets, he finally opted for a bottle of 2000 Chateau la Marzelle. The chateau had been the cause of much local debate when in 2006 it, and three other stalwarts of the Saint-Emilion classification aristocracy, had been demoted from premier grand cru classé status to the merely excellent grand cru classé. The assembly of the Jurade, who collectively check on each chateau in the appellation every decade, had been involved in a very modern *scandale*. "*Quelle aria!*" the locals had proclaimed. The jurats, with their extraordinary crimson robes and historic charter that dated from 1199 and King John, no less, stood accused of bribery and corruption, allowing personal interests and connections with the ever-powerful *négociants* to affect their palates. The effect of demotion was financially extraordinarily damaging and the grumbles from the four rusticated chateaux rumbled on even now. But for Starr the wine was still a fine one, marked by typical robust woodiness with notes of blackberry and old Armagnac in the finish. The tannins might need another few years to be fully integrated, but it was worth a try, Starr thought, and it would be robust enough to cope with the great Chateaubriand they had ordered.

Agnès was chatting when Starr's concentration was tugged away by shards of a conversation he could only just hear somewhere behind him. The voices were low and both male, and Starr caught initially single phrases "*note de suicide*" "*editeur de Cuvée*", "*scandale*", and then "*autopsie*".

"Have I lost you?" Agnès frowned at the distracted Starr.

"Sorry, sorry. I'm just going to the bathroom," he smiled reassuringly and hurriedly got up. He turned to identify the men who conversation had so intently interested him. Two contrasting figures were huddled in a corner table: one lined and drawn in a pleather biker's jacket, the other patrician, older, in a well-cut navy blue suit. Detective and *procureur*, he thought.

"Is everything alright, Monsieur Starr?" Madame Chabrol asked.

Starr took her by the elbow to the privacy of the restaurant's apparently empty interior. "Those two," he said jerking a thumb towards the door.

"Libourne police and the *procureur*," confirmed Madame Chabrol. "Why do they interest you?" But their conversation was cut short as the detective came in from the terrace.

"*Monsieur Starr, n'est ce pas?*" the detective rolled his 'rs'. "We need to arrange a time for your statement. It will be quite, how do you say, routine."

"Yes of course, *Commandant*. How did you know me?" Starr replied formally. The detective ignored the question and corrected him. "*Capitaine, monsieur.* You are here with Madame Janneau, the mother of the girl, yes?"

Starr lowered his voice so that Agnès couldn't hear. "Do you have the results of the autopsy?"

The detective smiled again. "I cannot discuss the case with you. Can you come to the gendarmerie tomorrow at 9.30. Is that too early for you?" Starr caught the slightest hint of sarcasm in the hard-boiled French arm of the law, but thought better of a cheap riposte. He needed to gain this man's trust and respect if he was ever to find the truth of what had happened at the Gothic arches.

"We'll be there at 9.30. *A demain*," Starr left the French investigators to their lunch and pushed through the doors to the toilettes at the back of the restaurant.

As he did so, he noticed a table of four men, all in suits, who had mysteriously chosen a table deep inside, while the brilliant spring sunshine sparkled on the terrace. They had two exceptional vintages on their table – either would have cost more than the price of his and Agnès' meal combined. Starr slowed his stride and tried to hear the conversation.

"Valentin, we have absolute faith in you," he heard. The speaker spoke in educated, upper class French.

"Business as usual then," he heard the man they called Valentin reply.

Starr was shown into the bland interview room by a uniformed gendarme. Erik Dacour was already waiting for him, tie loosened, the same dark rings under the blank eyes.

"I hope you understand that we have to interview each person separately," he said.

"Sure, of course," Starr nodded. Agnès seemed at least on the surface together enough to go through the inevitably prying questions about Sylvie's private life.

Starr repeated the facts as he knew them: Sylvie's job at *Cuvée*, the phone call suggesting they meet for dinner, the meal at Le Tertre, her account of the Romanée-Conti tasting at Damien Refeuille's office above the Trois Etoiles, the call from de Bachelet, the identification of the body. As Starr told his story into the police video recorder, the detective nodded, his face impassive.

"I know you think there has been, how do you say, err foul play," he started, "but I am glad to tell you that we are now sure Sylvie took her own life. Later today I have a meeting with the *procureur* and tomorrow morning we will formally release the body for burial," he said.

"What makes you so sure?" Starr felt the anger twist in his gut.

"The autopsy showed no sign of a struggle. Everything points to suicide. And she left a note," Dacour paused to let his statement have the impact he expected.

"What note? Where was the note?" Starr demanded.

"She left a note in her handbag. We didn't find it immediately because it was hidden in a side zip pocket. But it is certainly her writing and it was on Le Petit Girondine stationery. It explains why she took her life."

"Can I see it?"

"I can show you but I cannot release it until the *procureur* formally closes the case. It may help you accept the truth," he said kindly. He knocked on the plain door and whispered to the uniform outside it to bring the evidence bag.

The two men sat opposite each other in the empty room, without talking.

A gendarme placed the labelled transparent plastic bag with Sylvie's handbag in it down on the table.

"I know you don't believe she took her own life," Dacour said, "but I hope now you can begin to accept it."

"But, *Capitaine*, why would a girl who lives in Paris wait until she is here in Saint-Emilion and then...choose to do it like that? It makes no sense."

"Who can say *Monsieur?* She was very troubled, you know, in her private life. It is a tragedy, but one we have to accept."

"I can't accept it," Starr stared at the French detective. "She was murdered. I know she was."

"You know to hang a healthy young woman against her will is not a likely scenario for murder. Leave the proving to the authorities. It is better not to play Sherlock Holmes," Dacour said wearily.

"*Capitaine*, I am a simple American. I compile crosswords for a living. But Sylvie Janneau was my goddaughter. Her mother is one of my oldest friends. I will not allow you to relegate her life to a filing cabinet when somewhere out there in these vineyards a murderer walks free. I can't let this happen."

"I don't think it is a matter of choice, Monsieur. The law is the law," Dacour responded. "Perhaps when you see this note, it will make more sense."

The detective passed him a pair of gloves and then very carefully removed a folded piece of paper from the plastic evidence bag.

As Starr struggled to get his large hands into the powdery latex, Dacour told him that the handwriting had been examined by an expert, compared it to some extensive notes they had found in a notepad in her hotel room, and concluded it was genuine.

The letter was written on a crown quarto piece of hotel stationery from Le Petit Girondine. Starr tilted the paper against the light and could make out no indentations of a previous note from a pad. The paper was loose, he thought. There was neither a date nor an address nor was the letter directed to anyone in particular.

It read: "I am writing this to explain why I am going to end it all. I cannot stand the suffering any longer. My mother knows the reasons. Goodbye, goodbye, goodbye, Sylvie Janneau."

Starr read the note again. He took out his notebook and transcribed the words verbatim. Whatever doubts had troubled him before solidified like cooling wax into absolute certainty.

Looking up into the lined, bored face of the detective he said,

"This is a fake. I guarantee to you Sylvie could not have written it. There is no question at all and I will prove that to you," and with that he left the detective's office, knowing, no longer suspecting, that she had been murdered.

CHAPTER

3

S tarr was on the phone before he reached his car. Was it a decade, – more? – since he'd first met the precise and shy academic at some linguistics conference at the Four Seasons in New York? Whatever the timescale, he knew Bruno Le Blond would remember him.

"Vous avez joint la boîte vocale de Bruno Le Blond. Malheureusement je ne peux pas repondre a votre appel. Laissez-moi un message après les bips sonores."

"Christ!" Starr scrunched himself up like a piece of waste paper and threw himself into the driving seat of his faithful old Peugeot. His frustration was brought to an abrupt end as the familiar 'Take 5' ringtone rang on his cell.

"Hey Bruno – it's Franklin Starr here. Yes I know, it's been a while," he said.

"Ah Monsieur Starr, *comment ça va*? How is the world of crossed words?"

"Entangled," Starr replied, thinking 'Wet yarn I entangled (5)'. He didn't really like anagrams, but now and then they'd surface like sulphurous bubbles from the mud of his brain. Rainy. "Listen are you still working for the INPS?"

Le Blond had just joined the prestigious Institut National de Police Scientifique – France's version of the CSI crime labs – when the two men had met over a cigarette: a welcome escape from the deathly plenaries and breakaway sessions of a typically dreary academic conference. Nothing cements a friendship like a common enemy, thought Starr. Le Blond was a qualified graphologist – a discipline pretty much invented in France and although vilified by most of the world, still held in high esteem here in the hexagon. The rest of the world might think handwriting analysis akin to reading tea leaves but for the French it was a science as robust as Newton's law of gravity.

"Yes of course," replied Le Blond a little cagily. "In fact I am now the director of LPS 13's *écritures manuscrites* department," he added.

"Where's LPS 13?"

"Why Marseille."

"Can I come and see you – err – this afternoon?"

"*Calmez-vous, Monsieur Starr,* where is the fire?"

"I promise you this is extremely urgent," and Starr blurted out the salient details: the murder, his need to prove the note a fake before the Procureur confirmed poor Sylvie had taken her own life, the stubborn deafness of the French detective.

There was a long silence from the other end of the phone.

"Capitaine Dacour, you said, Libourne gendarmerie?"

"Look, Bruno, I need to jump on a plane – we haven't much time."

"It is better, I think, that I come to you. I need to see the paper, the ink, the spaces between the words. It is not just the words themselves, *vous comprenez Monsieur*? I will call you soon," and with that Le Blond rang off.

Starr was left with a feeling of relief on the one hand and apprehension on the other. On the plus side Le Blond was a qualified forensic graphologist, an *expert judiciaire*, whose opinion would weigh heavily with the police and the judiciary: on the other, he didn't seem to share Starr's sense of panic as time throbbed by. Would he make the effort to abandon his day just to indulge some American he met once at a conference?

They were like two spurs of a wishbone, thought Starr, meeting at a linguistic hinge. He'd spent his life playing with language, bending it, spinning it, revealing its geology, the layers of meaning laid down over centuries. Le Blond, however, interpreted the individuality of handwritten language, as expressions of a soul, as unique as a fingerprint and as incapable of forgery. For Starr the search for authenticity, for truth, was about holding the shifting sands of words in your mind at once, while for Le Blond it was a game of comparison, of spot the difference, to arrive at the truth through validation. Le Blond's truth was one of iteration: the more versions there were, the truer they must be. Starr's truth was more slippery: it existed somewhere between different interpretations, opposing magnetic forces. He was in danger of getting philosophical – seven days without a pun makes one weak.

Starr turned the old Peugeot onto the main road towards Saint-Emilion and took a left turn down a single-track lane that ran up into the vineyards sloping down towards the somnolent Dordogne that lay coiled at its base. The mists of the morning were finally lifting and the blue of the sky appeared to be deepening visibly in front of him. The road twisted sharply through the tiny stone villages and a campanile shattered the silence with a sudden clang of bells. It was midday.

The Lion d'Or wasn't a great restaurant but it was just what Starr needed. Its vine-covered terrace at the front of the old stone house wasn't even laid for lunch, but the *patronne* was soon rushing out to kiss Starr on each cheek holding a folded plastic tablecloth and cutlery under one arm. He ordered a vin blanc – a simple Bergerac sec – lit up a cigarette and got out his notebook. While his energies so far had been focused on getting the authorities to see that Sylvie had been murdered, his mind now turned to who might be her killer.

Starr shivered involuntarily as the still chill wind whipped round the terrace. Die of cold, he thought: 3, 4. Ice cube. First on his list was Gilles de Cazaux, *Cuvée's* editor. The affair between Sylvie and his wife would give him motive enough to get rid of the girl and what better opportunity than away from Paris among the vines of Saint-Emilion? Sylvie had said that he would follow her on Thursday, so he had opportunity. Starr made a note to check that de Cazaux had arrived for the *en primeur* tastings as planned. Next on his list was the unpleasant *négociant*, Damien Refeuille. How would a small *négociant* have access to some of the rarest and most sought-after vintages of any in the world and what was the story behind the dodgy Romanée-Conti '45 that Sylvie had identified as a fake?

Starr chewed on one of the fat black olives that Madame had brought out with his wine and made another note to call Jim Shawcross. If anyone could help him with Refeuille it was Jim.

Then, thought Starr, there might be others in Sylvie's life – a jealous ex, or some guy she'd rejected. After all, she was a seriously attractive girl. Had been, he corrected himself, as he turned to the blackboard displaying today's *menu du jour.*

He was tucking in to the garlic-roasted lamb and ratatouille when he felt his cellphone vibrate in his pocket.

Mouth full, he answered "Starr," and swallowed hard. It was Agnès.

"Where are you? I have just had a call from Gilles de Cazaux," her voice trembled slightly.

"I'm just finishing a quick lunch," Starr replied a little guiltily and not quite accurately. "Wait at the house and I'll be there in under half an hour."

As he negotiated the narrow lanes that took him over the top of the hills near Saussignac, he caught an immense view of the fields spread below. The blankets of vineyards were here and there marked by a square-towered chateau or a little, round stone-tiled windmill. Some way in the distance the characteristic narrow tractor of the vineyards was making its way between the rows of vine stumps, its old blue paint gleaming in the sunshine like a small beetle. Starr couldn't explain what it was about this ancient landscape that still, after all these years, made him catch his breath. His spirits lifted as he turned the smoky old Peugeot onto his gravel drive. Agnès emerged through the kitchen door.

"Why is he calling me? Franklin," those rolling French 'r's tumbling like rocks in a stream, "I am scared."

"Why Agnès?" Starr put a paternal arm around his old friend's shoulders. "It's natural that he should be in touch, and it could be a good opportunity to quiz him, apply some pressure."

Agnès frowned and wrinkled her nose in enquiry.

"I'm going to get us some coffee," said Starr. "And we can talk on the terrace."

They sat at either end of the old stone table, like matching bookends, each warming their hands around Starr's handleless mugs. Starr wasn't sure how much of his thinking to share with Agnès. She was still struggling to come to terms with her daughter's suicide. How would she cope when, and Starr thought it must be when not if, it was confirmed she'd been brutally murdered. In the end he decided to compromise and told her that he'd called the forensic graphologist and he might help with Sylvie's note.

Agnès shook her head. "You won't give up," she said. "You always were provocative." Starr smiled. Provocative from the Latin *provocare* – to call forth – he hoped he would prove worthy of the epithet.

As if in response, a faint rumble announced the arrival of a well-tuned engine and a black BMW 7 Series swung rather too quickly into the smallish driveway stopping just short of the back of Starr's battered old Peugeot. Starr couldn't see the driver through the privacy glass and was half way to the car when the familiar voice shouted, at full volume: "Starr – you here? I've brought you a jammy little Lagrange 2002. Get us a corkscrew, there's a good lad," the bottle with its creamy label bearing an engraving of the elegant single-towered chateau was followed by the bulky frame of Jim Shawcross extricating itself with difficulty from the sleek German car. As Starr dived into the gloom of his kitchen in search of glasses and corkscrew, he looked over his shoulder to see Shawcross unsuccessfully smoothing down his thick unruly hair as he crossed over to the terrace where Agnès was waiting. Starr had never asked Shawcross about his personal circumstances and only then realised he had no idea whether the burly old rascal was even married.

A few minutes later Starr was opening the highly-rated Saint-Julien on the stone table and noting Agnès' faultless manners as she laughed at all Jim's dreadful jokes.

"I see you've introduced yourselves," he said.

Agnès laughed in response and freed her leonine head of blond hair from the old Hermès scarf she often wore, Grace Kelly style.

"Have you seen this?" Shawcross shoved a copy of the *Sud-Ouest* over the table towards Starr. With the interview at the gendarmerie and everything else he hadn't even glanced at the paper today. It was in the *Faits Divers* section: a photo of the ruined convent arches still cordoned off and a headshot of Dacour. Fortunately the paper had not got hold of a photo of Sylvie and the report was quite short confirming suspected suicide. Starr jumped in before Shawcross could put his large Lancastrian foot in it.

"Yes it's the most terrible tragedy: Agnès' daughter, Sylvie. She is – was – my goddaughter, Jim."

"Christ, Franklin, I had no idea. I've not heard you mention her? I'm intruding, so sorry," and he got up to go.

"No please, Monsieur Shawcross," Agnès replied, her otherwise good English snagging on the difficult 'r'.

"Call me Jim – everyone does."

"Jeem, Please stay. Nothing will bring Sylvie back and life, you know, must go on. Franklin cannot accept she took her own life, but perhaps you can reason with him," she added.

Shawcross stretched over to one of the glasses and raised it solemnly. "Veritas," he said. "Here's to the truth."

The dark red-black wine, restrained austerity on the nose with a black cherry core, was indeed jammy, thought Starr. The sooty black fruits were overlaid with a wave of sweet violets and the finish was all blackberries but not at all overdone, the tannin lingering just long enough.

"Mmmm," said Shawcross. "I quite like these Lagranges. What do you think Starr?"

"Great," Starr said. "Bulging with fruit but restrained somehow. Sort of sweet-sour."

"That's well put," Shawcross said.

"It reminds me of violets," Agnès joined in the discussion. Jim turned to look at her and Starr thought they locked eyes just a fraction longer than necessary.

Agnès said she was getting cold and went in to the house to get herself a cardigan.

"Now what are we going to do about Sylvie Janneau's murder," Shawcross said abruptly, raising both hairy eyebrows and looking straight at Starr.

No-one was more surprised than Starr to find Shawcross agreeing with him – after all, he knew nothing about the bum suicide note. "What makes you sure she didn't hang herself?" he asked.

"Oh come on. A young woman in her mid-20s, a rising star at *Cuvée*, a Master of Wine at an impossibly precocious age. Gets the train from Paris to report on the *en primeur*tastings, sees a few chateaux owners, has dinner with a *négociant* and then clambers onto some wine crates, puts a rope round her neck and says *au revoir*. Nah. I'm not buying," he said.

"How did you know all that?" Starr took another gulp of the ripe cherry Lagrange.

"You bloody Americans think you're the only people in the universe with a brain in their skulls," said Shawcross. "I got a call from de Bachelet. Think it rattled him a bit. He found the body, you know."

"Actually he didn't find it – it was one of his guys walking his dog. The police got him there because his was the last number she called – on her cell. He called me and I was next there. They'd already cut her down, but not by long," Starr shuddered.

"So now what? What are you doing?" persisted Shawcross.

"Err... I've called a guy I know in the French crime labs; he's a graphologist, handwriting expert you know. I figure if I can get him to testify the suicide note's a fake, then at least there will be an investigation," Starr was talking fast, aware that Agnès would be back in minutes.

"Suicide note? She left a note?"

Starr took his notebook out of his jacket pocket and showed Shawcross the transcription he'd made in the interview room earlier that morning.

"Load of bollocks," said Shawcross. "Goodbye, goodbye, goodbye. Who writes that?"

At that moment both men fell silent as Agnès joined them again, a grey-blue cardigan hanging from her shoulders and her lipstick freshly applied. Looking from side to side at Starr and Shawcross she said,

"OK If someone murdered Sylvie I want to find out who and I want him to rot in jail for all his miserable life." She then took a large swallow of wine and Starr noticed the determined set of her jaw and the impossible iris-blue of her eyes.

As Shawcross wrestled himself into his car again, he said, by way of explanation.

"It's a hire car. I tell the girls in the office I want something basic, but they don't listen. They think I actually enjoy pratting about in some over-engineered boat. We should swap! Don't forget to call me. I just might be able to help, you know," and with that he reversed the BMW at alarming speed almost into one of La Borie's stone gateposts before turning and disappearing up the lane.

"Now there is an English gentleman," said Agnès to the dusty cloud that hovered over the gravel.

"You reckon?" Starr was doubtful.

"Pure solid gold," she said twirling the last of her wine in the glass.

Starr's cellphone beeped to tell him he'd missed a call and checking the log he saw that it was Le Blond. "I gotta make this call," he apologised and loped off across the lawn hoping for good news.

"*Monsieur Starr, bonjour,*" said Le Blond slightly hesitantly. "It seems that the handwriting has already been *verifié*. The autopsy is unequivocal too. There is nothing I can do. I am sorry," he added.

"No Bruno. Please Bruno. Come and see the note."

"*Impossible, désolé,*" and he rang off.

Starr's heart sank.

It was now nearly four o'clock and Dacour had said the hearing would be the next day. If the Procureur declared suicide the "*obstacle médico-légale à l'inhumation*" would be lifted and the body returned to the family for burial. Now that Agnès doubted Sylvie's suicide, Starr thought he could persuade her to hold off the funeral, but keeping the body intact and unembalmed presented practical difficulties, and that was essential to finding out what had really happened.

Starr left Agnès watching TV and drove to Libourne. He had one shot and it was, as he thought, his last.

Men in blue were the same the world over, thought Starr, as he was met with the dead, blank stare of the duty sergeant. "I've seen it all before," his look told him, "And I ain't budging."

"Inspector Dacour asked me to drop by the office," Starr improvised. "Could you perhaps dial his extension?" he smiled encouragingly. The sergeant remained immobile.

Then something miraculous happened. Through the security door that led down the corridor to Dacour's office, came a youngish police woman. She was wearing a T-shirt under her holster and black jeans. She had glossy dark hair cut short. As she was about to leave the station, she turned and asked Starr what he wanted. It turned out she had taken Agnès' statement, but that wasn't all.

"Tof," she called to the slab of police meat at the desk. "Dial Erik's number please. He is waiting to see this err person," she added vaguely. The meat mountain reluctantly dialled. Starr was in.

She held the security door open for him and escorted him to Erik Dacour's bureaucratic cave. As Starr turned to thank her he just caught Dacour raise his shoulders, spread both hands out, palms to heaven. "What the hell?" it said, but no words came from his mouth. The female gendarme shrugged back and grinned at the bad-tempered detective as she closed the door on the two men.

"Monsieur Starr. You must stop now. No more, how do you say, *ingérance*, interference," the irritation in his voice showed through like a flash of underpants.

"*Comment?*" Starr feigned ignorance.

"LPS 13, *Monsieur Le Blond*. This is *insupportable, Monsieur,* and it will not change anything."

Starr wasn't sure if it was the detective's ego, his love of protocol or Starr's pulling a rabbit the size of Le Blond out of his hat that had irritated the detective the most. In reality it was probably a mix of all three. He decided to be conciliatory.

"Look I'm sorry," he started. "But I have to be sure. You would do the same if it was your, err, daughter. You got kids, *Capitaine?*"

"No kids."

"Ah, well me neither. But the fact is she was a young woman at the start of her life. She deserves a proper investigation," Starr warmed to his theme.

"There is nothing to investigate," said Dacour wearily, as if explaining something very simple to a dull child for the hundredth time.

"Look. I just want one favour," Starr said. "Scan the original suicide note and send it as a high res jpeg to Bruno Le Blond. That can't hurt, can it?"

The detective felt his well-grown stubble along either side of his jawline with his fingertips and stared at Starr. Starr wasn't sure what he was thinking, but it seemed to take an uncomfortable age.

"If I send a scan," he said finally, "And Monsieur Le Blond confirms the opinion of our expert, do I have your word you will stop?"

Starr thought for a split second, then he nodded.

Dacour hit a buzzer under his desk and a secretary appeared. He gave her instructions to bring the evidence bag and rose to shake Starr's hand. The meeting was over. The secretary returned, handed over the bag to the inspector and led Starr down the linoleum corridor that smelt of disinfectant to the police station entrance.

Outside in the fresh air, Starr lit up and inhaled deeply as with his other hand he texted Le Blond. Best to keep it short, he thought, as he fumbled with the touchscreen. Sauntering off to find his car parked under the pollarded plane trees in front of the gendarmerie, he was stopped by the T-shirted police woman who came running down the steps towards him.

"*Monsieur*," she said. " Have you a moment?" she asked. "Not here," turning a little anxiously to the blank windows of the police station.

"Sure. Can I buy you a drink?" Starr was curious on several levels.

"What can I get you...err, sorry I don't know your name?" asked Starr as they sat down at the back of a narrow little café round the corner from the police station. He'd never had a thing about women in uniform and of course the woman settling herself across the small round table from him was not in uniform per se, but there was a certain thrill... his thoughts lay in pieces as she broke in,

"A *tisane*. Christiane Montreux."

"Oh OK, *bonjour Madame Montreux. Enchanté.* Any particular tea?"

"*Un vert jasmine*, if they have it," she replied.

The surly waitress was in no rush to take their order or to deliver it to her red-faced colleague behind the bar.

"I understand you have some difficulties, is that right, with the suicide explanation for the death of Sylvie Janneau?"

Starr looked at the intelligent face of Christiane Montreux, her dark brown eyes unflinching, and decided to entrust his hand to hers and be led down an unknown path.

"No difficulty," he replied. "I know for a fact she was murdered. I know she could never have written that note, that it's a complete fake. And if she didn't write it then who did?"

"What are your reasons to be so sure?"

Starr took his battered notebook from his inside jacket pocket and opened it at the page of the transcription. He showed her the message:

'I am writing this to explain why I am going to end it all. I cannot stand the suffering any longer. My mother knows the reasons. Goodbye, goodbye, goodbye, Sylvie Janneau.'

"First this letter is not dated and it is not addressed to anyone – strange surely. Second, it is full of clichés: 'end it all', 'cannot stand the suffering'. Sylvie Janneau was an editor – well-educated and used to using language professionally. These are not the words of an expert communicator. Then she mentions her mother but not directly. Not 'Maman, you know why I have to do this' but in the third person. Who is the letter addressed to? Then there is the ridiculous melodramatic 'goodbye' repeated three times and finally the signature. Not Sylvie but Sylvie Janneau. No, it is a weak attempt at a faked suicide note and I know she could not have written it."

"Oh, you are an expert in the language of suicide notes?" asked Christiane Montreux frowning attractively.

"Fortunately not," said Starr. "But I am a crossword compiler and that makes me quite sensitive to language, I think. Anyway, why did you want to see me?"

"Please call me Christiane," the woman's tone became grave.

"There is something I should not tell you. It may cost me my job. But I have no-one to share this with and I think it may be important. It may not, of course..." her voice drifted off.

"Go on," Starr encouraged her, feeling the hairs on the back of his neck prickle.

"The *portable* that was there at the scene – verified by two police reports and the Procureur's *adjointe* (his deputy) – is missing. It never got into the evidence bag. When I mentioned it to Erik Dacour he was angry. I had to swear to say nothing about it. He says it would make the centre look careless and just create a *brouhaha* for nothing. But it is so rare for something to go missing, especially a telephone."

Starr was intrigued and about to question Christiane when his own frigging phone rang. It was Le Blond but on an atrocious line.

"Concerns...cannot judge from the digital copy... Procureur... agreed delay...tomorrow 12.40 at Mérignac," then he hung up.

"I believe, Christiane, we are not the only ones to have doubts. That was the head of the écritures manuscrites of INPS Marseille and he is flying into Bordeaux tomorrow to take a look at that suicide note for himself."

The faintest shadow momentarily crossed the police detective's face.

Starr took a large gulp of the tea he hated and looked out across the almost empty café to the busy street outside where people were already queuing up at the bakeries for their evening baguettes.

CHAPTER

4

Starr woke as the early blush of dawn glowed in the misty horizon, after an excellent night's sleep – his first for a while. Le Blond was due into Mérignac airport a bit after midday and there was nothing pressing to do before that. He got out of bed and performed his 11-minute exercise routine. It hadn't changed in over 20 years and was originally designed for the Canadian Air Force back in the fifties – not that he went back quite that far. Starr liked it because it was short and needed no equipment. It started with touching your toes and ended with running on the spot. The worst part were the push-ups in the middle. His sacrifice to Salus, the health goddess, completed, he showered and dressed and clattered down the old oak stairs.

He took a cafetière of coffee, a large bowl, a cinnamon stick, his cellphone, yesterday's *Sud-Ouest*, a plastic supermarket bag, iPad and notebook onto the terrace. Shoving the plastic bag under his bony bottom to protect it from the dew-drenched stone bench, he poured his first coffee of the day into the bowl, floated the cinnamon stick on top and opened the *Sud-Ouest* at the report on Sylvie's death. He wrote down the journalist's name from the byline in his notebook and also the name of the *adjointe* – the Procureur's assistant who had attended the scene.

Waking up his iPad, he opened the XWord studio program he'd recently downloaded and decided on a regular 15 x 15 grid. Starr was both a traditionalist and an Anglophile when it came to crosswords. He believed the greatest compilers were British and the greatest clues came from that damp little island. It went with other British strengths – devising games although not playing them very well, puns and jokes, code-breaking, spying and detective fiction. A land of deception, thought Starr, where dark, but not very serious, arts thrived in the drizzly gloom. Let's not forget, thought Starr warming to his theme, the word's Greek roots – *kryptikos* – 'fit for concealing', from *kryptos* 'hidden' also giving us 'crypt.'

Starr had just finished what he thought was a half-decent clue when Agnès appeared in her robe and looked over his shoulder at the semi-completed grid on his screen.

"Bill goes to the North gate (7)," she read. "I don't get it."

"Hmm?" Starr was still swimming in the depths of double meanings and etymologies. "Oh, postern. The bill is a poster plus 'n' for North."

"Ah, now I see how it works," Agnès said shaking her head and poured herself a bowl of coffee. Her languid stare out across the spectacular view abruptly altered.

"Franklin, I didn't call Gilles de Cazaux yesterday. Should I do it today do you think?"

"Hmm?" Starr was still not paying attention.

"Gilles – Sylvie's editor – I think I must call him. Don't you agree?"

"Sorry. I'll put it away. Finish it later." He powered down the iPad and turned to focus on his old friend.

"De Cazaux called?"

"Yes, I told you. Yesterday just before *midi*. Remember?"

With all that had happened – his fruitless efforts with Le Blond and then the last-minute recapitulation, the story of the missing phone, meeting Christiane Montreux – he'd forgotten all about de Cazaux.

"Yes call him," Starr checked his watch to see whether it was still too early.

"Let me get dressed first," said Agnès. "And then I will do it, but I want you to listen," and with that she took her coffee into the house.

Agnès dialled the number on Starr's landline, there being no signal in the house or immediate garden. You could sometimes, if you were lucky, get one bar up a few stone steps the far side of La Borie's lawn, which was in reality more of a field, but not reliably. Starr put his head close to Agnès' so they could both hear the conversation without alerting de Cazaux by putting it on speakerphone.

The call was short and business-like. Agnès would meet the smart editor at the even smarter Hostellerie de Plaisance – Saint-Emilion's five star hotel positioned slap bang next to the Eglise Monolithe's bell tower. From it there was an unbeatable view over the cobbled square below and the 12th century King's Tower, where, every third Sunday of June and September, the jurade, in their crimson robes, repeated the ancient oath to defend the reputation of Saint-Emilion and its vineyards. Typical, thought the democrat Starr. De Cazaux *would* stay at the flashy Plaisance.

Agnès had dressed in an old Chanel tweed suit she'd had for years, but that fitted her perfectly and a cashmere sweater that matched her violet eyes.

"Do I need to change?" Starr asked as she appeared in the kitchen.

"Perhaps a jacket and proper shoes," advised Agnès looking down at Starr's battered old trainers. He galloped up the stairs three at a time and was back in a few minutes, shod for the Hostellerie de Plaisance and the exotic de Cazaux.

As the old Peugeot approached the little town, you got a perfect view of its shape, built into a natural amphitheatre in the limestone hillside, and clustered up its hillside, a three-dimensional puzzle in white stone. No wonder, thought Starr, the Benedictine monks had chosen to site the town there.

De Cazaux was to be found, as he promised, in the drawing room of the Plaisance, reading *Le Figaro*, his elegant legs crossed, his Aubercy shoes polished, a tray with a caffetière of coffee on the table next to him. Opposite him was an older man, also reading. As they drew near, Starr realised it was the man from the back of La Belvédère.

De Cazaux stood up and kissed Agnès three times. His handshake with Starr was firm, while the hand was soft and manicured. Then he introduced the man opposite who had also risen from his chair.

"Agnès, I don't know if you know our famous wine editor, Valentin Charpentier?" Starr was clearly superfluous to this dance of introductions, but it suited him to stand and watch from the reserve bench.

Agnès smiled and said *"Enchantée"* as Valentin Charpentier excused himself and sauntered off through the glass double doors out of the hotel lounge to the reception lobby beyond.

The elegant room was flooded with light through the arched windows and, it being *en primeur* season, there was the buzz of a full hotel.

De Cazaux was exceptionally good-looking: medium-height, tanned, athletic, his dark brown hair swept naturally away from his temples, his dark eyes large and fringed by thick, long lashes. He carefully removed and folded his designer round tortoiseshell glasses and put them on top of the newspaper.

"I am so very sorry for your loss," he said to Agnès, apparently genuinely, and then, addressing both of them, continued, "Would you prefer to speak in French or English?" while motioning to a hotel waiter to refresh the coffee tray.

"Perhaps English, so that my American friend Monsieur Starr, can easily follow," said Agnès, a little mischievously Starr thought, since he didn't think his French was much worse than Agnès' English.

"Your editor, Monsieur Charpentier," Starr's voice sounded too loud, too urgent. He attempted to muffle it.

"Does he always come for the *en primeur*?"

"Well naturally. *Cuvée* publishes a 'top 20' list of each vintage's best wines. It is one of our hallmarks, what we are known for, and Valentin, he is perhaps the world's greatest wine writer, and now, of course a *jurat*. There is no-one, not even your famous Mr Parker, who does not take notice of his list," de Cazaux flashed a warm, patronising, confident smile in the general direction of Starr, without really looking at him.

"You were Sylvie's godfather, I understand," de Cazaux continued, getting down to the matter in hand.

"Yeah, not a very good one, but I was very proud of her," Starr said.

"We all were, I think," said de Cazaux. "She was an exceptional young editor, you know, and in all my career at *La Cuvée* I have not met another with her passion for wine."

Agnès was studying the polished parquet, getting a grip, thought Starr.

"So you wanted to talk to Agnès?" he asked.

"Yes...well...I wanted to offer my condolences, you know. My wife and I had become very – attached – to Sylvie. She was one of the family. She came to us often to our country place at Charly-sur-Marne on weekends. My wife was particularly...err...close," he said. "We had no idea, really no clue, that she was...*triste, déprimé.*"

Starr had agreed with Agnès they would not share anything they knew about Sylvie's death – most particularly that they believed she had been murdered, since de Cazaux remained high on the list of suspects.

"Who knows what was in her heart," said Agnès, now fully composed.

"So you did not know of any cause, any reason for this?" de Cazaux pressed her.

"Did *you?*" Agnès said with the force of a mother bear.

"Ah no. Of course not."

A silence fell on the group of three as they all drank from the Plaisance's polite china with its pretentious gold crest.

To break the silence, Starr said, "I had dinner with her, here in Saint-Emilion, on Wednesday night. She was a woman in bloom," he said, surprised by the florid language that had crept in, uninvited.

"So you saw her the night before she...err"

"Yes," interjected Starr, "And she was very well."

There was another slightly awkward pause before de Cazaux spoke.

"Did she...did she, by any chance, mention having met a négociant by the name of Refeuille?" de Cazaux was trying to sound airy, but was clearly intensely interested.

Starr frowned and bought himself a few seconds' thinking time. How much did de Cazaux know? How could he best find out?

"No... I can't say she did. Who is he?" Starr lied.

"To be honest, I do not know. He operates from here, in Saint-Emilion. Sylvie met him at one of the chateaux tastings. She...sent me a message, a text, saying something about having been offered a Romanée-Conti '45 at his office. You may not know," de Cazaux was getting into his stride now, "But this is one of the greatest vintages of all time and no known bottles are left, so it was very surprising."

Starr smiled and played the dumb American, so de Cazaux continued.

"Sylvie suggested there was something wrong with the wine. She gave very few details. Probably nothing," he drifted off. "I expect the police have investigated, anyway," he added as an afterthought.

"So," said Starr brightly, "When did you get here?"

"Me?" asked de Cazaux as though there were several candidates for Starr's question.

"I got the early TGV on Thursday morning – I will probably return tomorrow. I decided to stay on just to hear the Procureur's formal announcement," he added, not letting on whether or not he knew it had been delayed.

"And Valentin Charpentier, did he travel with you?"

"Really, Mr Starr, you sound like a policeman with all your questions. No, Valentin likes to drive – his most prized possession, apart from his Roederer Awards – is his Mercedes S-Class. Paris affords him few opportunities to indulge his passion, so he always drives here. He has been here since Monday night, I believe."

"Sorry to sound nosy," said Starr feebly. De Cazaux ignored him and turned to Agnès.

"Madame Janneau, if there is anything the magazine can do to assist in the funeral arrangements, we would be delighted to play some small part," he said. And with that he rose, extracted two claret-coloured business cards from his typically French little leather man bag, and presented them in turn to Agnès and then to Starr. "My *co-ordinées* are all there," he said.

Just as Starr and Agnès were leaving Starr had a final thought.

"Monsieur de Cazaux, do you still have that text message about the wine from Sylvie?"

"Err yes, I believe so," de Cazaux replied.

"Would you mind very much showing me?"

"Well...I...ah, *domage*," he said. "It is on my other *portable*. In Paris. *Je suis desolé, Monsieur.*"

"Ah, *tant pis*," Starr continued. "Perhaps you should keep that text safe, you know, in case it is important," and with that he put a steering hand on Agnès' left elbow and the two left the Hostellerie de Plaisance, with more questions than answers.

Starr checked his watch. It was 11.50.

"Go, Franklin. Don't be late," urged Agnès. "I will see you back at La Borie this evening."

Starr watched Agnès' trim figure, her left hand raised in a farewell wave, as she disappeared down the chemin des Fossés. She didn't really look like an academic, thought Starr, but then she didn't look like a business woman or a *potiche*, a trophy wife, either. She was meeting an old colleague from the Musée de l'Homme who was writing the ultimate work on the Hottentot Venus, or so she had told him. He would give her a lift back to La Borie, leaving Starr free.

Starr got onto the autoroute at Libourne and negotiated the various junctions that surrounded Bordeaux to get out west to Mérignac. Signs to Cap Ferret and Arcachon reminded him that he must take Anaïs to the bassin at the base of the majestic dune Pyla for a long lunch of oysters, before the weather warmed up and they were no longer at their best.

He parked the old car in the short term area of the car-park that was a few yards from the main terminal building and strode into the arrivals hall. According to the board, the Air France flight from Marseilles was on time. Starr sat down on one of the space-age style benches and wrote in his notebook. He must remember to tell Dacour about Sylvie's text message to de Cazaux. Perhaps there were other text messages from her? Perhaps there was evidence that he knew about his wife's affair? Was Valentin Charpentier significant? Lunch with chateau owners at the Belvédère was innocent enough, but who drinks €300 wines at lunchtime and sits in the dark when the sun is blazing on a terrace with perhaps the best view of any restaurant in Aquitaine?

A small, neat Le Blond came through the automatic door. He was carrying a large briefcase and wore a grey suit and tie and a Burberry trenchcoat. He was wearing round steel-rimmed glasses and had a small moustache. In fact he was exactly as Starr remembered him from a decade ago. He raised his eyebrows in recognition of the tall American and the two men walked silently to Starr's waiting car.

"I'm so glad you are here – that you agreed to come," said Starr.

Le Blond did not answer immediately.

"Listen, Monsieur, I think it prudent we do not discuss any matters relating to Sylvie Janneau's death," he said finally.

"Sure, OK," said Starr. A retriever bounded across the car park in front of him followed by a gaggle of kids whistling and calling him back.

"A fetching breed of dog," said Starr, but he wasn't sure if Le Blond caught the joke.

It was a tense journey to Libourne. Starr made a few feeble attempts at small talk, but his head was full of only one thing, and that was the thing he couldn't discuss. He'd seen the sense in going along with Le Blond. After all, for his opinion to carry maximum weight with Dacour and more importantly, the Procureur, it needed to be absolutely objective. The three men were all part of the same team, the same system of French justice, albeit playing different positions and Starr had no place on the pitch.

He accompanied Le Blond up the gendarmerie's front steps and introduced him to the Duty Sergeant. Le Blond turned and shook his hand formally as if to say 'you can go now' but Starr thought he saw just a hint of collusion in his face, the faintest smile around the bespectacled eyes.

The afternoon sun was now surprisingly hot and Starr was glad to dump his jacket, loosen the top few buttons of his shirt and unbutton his cuffs so they flapped around his wrists. He needed something to take his mind off what was happening in the Libourne gendarmerie and decided to drive to Saint-Emilion, install himself in one of the few little cafés guaranteed not to be filled with Japanese tourists and attempt to finish off his crossword.

There was a small place to the east of the town, just inside the Porte Brunet – the only one of the six original medieval gates that still survived. Its stark 12th century stone walls were a reminder of what would have been a massive fortified city wall, all made from limestone quarried from within the hill itself and to this day leaving 200 kilometres of interconnected tunnels. The tunnels had provided secret escape routes to generations of Girondins from those caught on the wrong side of the 100 years war to the French Revolution and German occupation. They were used to this day, for who knows what nefarious activities.

There was a shabby little courtyard with a simple fountain and some overgrown climbing plants that were just sprouting into life. Starr chose a table in the shade and spread himself out. He ordered a large pot of coffee and a Croque and stretched out his legs under the wrought iron table. A tortoiseshell cat was sunbathing, curled up and completely filling a flower-pot, a terracotta cat basket. As Starr waited for the coffee to arrive he thought of the first time he had come to Saint-Emilion. It had been in the fall just before the *vendange*, the vineyards glowing yellow in the low October sun. He would never forget the sudden blindness on entering the Eglise Monolithe – with its crumbling limestone pillars, enormous spaces and strange pagan wall paintings: the man wrestling a dragon with four snakes on his back.

On the door to the church, you could still just make out the original plan for the town. The Benedictine monks had drawn on much older, thoroughly pagan principles for its shape and structure. Erecting a tall pole at the water source – that was always the starting point – idea was to mirror a section of the sky and by following the pole's shadow as the sun moved across the sky, the city limits were drawn by a ploughshare. The gates corresponded to celestial gates – to constellations. From memory, Brunet was under the sign of Scorpio.

Starr thought how even in these digital, high-tech times, ancient forces were still at work. For all the science that goes into contemporary wine-making for example, biodynamic viticulture is on the rise. There were serious wine-makers devoted to a system where organic principles meet the spiritual, with all the voodoo of lunar cycles, burying soil in cow's horns and the rest of it. Even the most erudite *oenologue* stops short of dismissal when it comes to the effects of sun and moon, of astrological forces on the alchemy that turns a humble grape into the poetry of a fine vintage wine.

Starr opened his iPad and was thinking of a clue for 'cremates' when his coffee and Croque arrived. 'Burn 'em in boxes' might work, he thought.

He was lost in the outer reaches of the Crossworders' Dictionary and Gazeteer, when snatches of a one-sided conversation caught his attention.

It was a male voice, speaking on a cellphone, animated and a little secretive at the same time. Starr heard something about shipping, wine-tasting, the InterContinental Hong Kong, the need to pack the bottles carefully in straw, not to forget the *capsules de bouchage* and the *bouchons*, payment as usual. The conversation ended.

Why was it odd? Négociants and chateaux-owners had been wooing new markets in China for decades now, and high-profile wine-tasting events in Hong Kong, Shanghai and Beijing were commonplace. It was the bit about not forgetting the corks and the metal foil that covered them that struck a wrong note.

Starr's curiosity on alert, he extricated his legs from under the table and lighting a cigarette walked towards the source of the conversation. A small alley led out of the back of the courtyard and just at its far end he caught sight of a figure, silhouetted against the still-bright sun, turn into the street. Starr thought he recognised something about his longish hair, but failed to place him.

Back at his table, his phone flashed 'missed call' and opening the menu he saw it was a number he didn't recognise or have in his contacts. He dialled.

"Dacour," the detective was clipped and charmless.

"You called me, Detective," said Starr. "This is Franklin Starr."

"Ah oui, merci," Dacour sounded almost friendly. "Can you come to the gendarmerie? Are you with Madame Janneau perhaps? We would like to discuss some new developments."

Starr's heart bust against his ribs as he drove much too fast the six kilometres or so from Saint-Emilion to Libourne.

As he swung the old white Peugeot into the cobbled car park in front of the station, he almost collided with Christiane Montreux, this time in her dark blue gendarme uniform, the pillar box hat pulled down low, the brim only just above her eyes. She waved as she recognised him before walking purposefully over to a waiting police car that drove off at speed.

The large sweaty cop at the desk was the same guy that had been there yesterday, but what a difference a day makes, thought Starr.

He was on the phone before Starr could introduce himself and gesturing him towards a security door on the opposite side to the corridor that led to Dacour's office. A young gendarme opened the door and led Starr to a large, bright meeting room. Here Dacour, Le Blond and a third man were all talking quietly together. The third man was the first to turn and greet Starr.

"*Philippe Giraud, Procureur.*"

He was balding and in his early sixties, wearing a suit, tie, glasses and wedding ring: a man with no distinguishing features, instantly forgettable. But when he spoke, you listened.

"Thank you for coming to the station," he said. "We are all very grateful. I understand that Madame Janneau is not currently *disponible*?"

"I have left her a voicemail message but she may be out of range."

"As a close friend of the family, I will share with you some new developments that have arisen concerning the investigation into the causes of the death of Sylvie Janneau."

Starr looked at Le Blond who had the ability to pull a blind down over his face, shutting out any trace of what might be happening inside. It left Starr none the wiser.

"*Monsieur Dacour, Capitaine,* chief investigator in this case, sought a second opinion on the authenticity of the suicide note found in Sylvie Janneau's effects. Monsieur Le Blond is one of France's most eminent *graphologistes,* and heads the Marseille *laboratoire d'écritures manuscrites* of the *Institut National de Police Scientifique.* After a forensic examination of the letter apparently written by Madamoiselle Janneau before she took her own life, I, as public Procureur in this case, working closely with my two esteemed colleagues here, have concluded that the letter is not by her hand. As a result, we have to conclude that, in spite of the autopsy results, this is not a suicide. Today I have instigated a murder investigation. I am very sorry, Monsieur Starr."

He handed Starr two stiff white business cards, embossed with raised black copperplate type, with his name and telephone numbers. "Please give my card to Madame Janneau and pass on my *sentiments distingués*. She is welcome to contact me at any time."

The Procureur turned to Dacour who said, "I am indebted, Monsieur Starr, to your help in this matter. Please remain in the area. We will certainly want to interview again yourself and Madame Janneau, now that the nature of our enquiry has changed."

The Procureur asked Le Blond to accompany him to some other office down the passageway, leaving Dacour alone in the meeting room with Starr.

"Cigarette?" he asked, and the two men walked together down the corridor and out into the late afternoon sunshine.

CHAPTER

5

T he house seemed strangely empty now that Agnès had returned to Paris. Suddenly the lack of a second mug, a handbag on the table or a pair of shoes left kicked off by the sofa, left a tangible emptiness as if the place they had once occupied remained reserved, as solid negative spaces. Anaïs never stayed long enough to make a lasting impression on the surface of Starr's well-worn life, but Agnès had fully inhabited La Borie, much like Esmé had done during their 15-year-long and happy marriage, before cancer intervened.

Agnès was anxious to get home, to go back to her desk in the quai Branly, and the meticulous work she loved. While the home of the Musée de l'Homme was undergoing its two-year renovation, she had been leading a team of specialist conservateurs re-evaluating the hundreds of thousands of artefacts held in the collection. It would have driven Starr mad with boredom but it was the kind of fastidious, detailed work Agnès adored.

No doubt, he thought, Dacour would be off to Paris to search Sylvie's flat as soon as he'd got the press conference over and there would be a whole new set of questions for Agnès to help with.

Starr decided to indulge in a rare and long bath. It was a week since Sylvie had been murdered and Agnès and he had given two more interviews to the police. Fingerprints had been taken and Starr had offered a mouth swab for his DNA. It hadn't occurred to him that he'd be a suspect until Dacour had asked him that quintessential cliché of police investigations.

He had been at home on Thursday evening and as usual, was alone. As luck would have it, though, he'd lent his car to a wily, old vigneron called Viremoneix who lived down his lane and was pursuing an unlikely but seemingly torrid affair with a barmaid in Sainte Foy la Grande. The old devil hadn't returned it until the morning, an hour before he knew Starr would be up. While Starr had no alibi, his car did, and that seemed to satisfy Dacour. Also, thought Starr as he sank below the warm water, what murderer would have been so insistent on upturning the police's initial verdict of suicide.

Starr's sybaritic indulgence was short-lived. He was pleasantly marinating in the hot water when he heard the crunch of his gravel driveway, slamming doors and voices.

He was dressed and downstairs in a few minutes, his thick just greying hair wet and uncharacteristically slicked neat against his scalp.

"Ah, Monsieur," shouted the now familiar figure of M. Acrylic Jumper. Pointing to his companion and then to the roof, with all the subtlety of a pantomime dame, he simply said, *"Pour les guêpes."*

Starr had forgotten all about the apparent hornets' nest under his roof but, squinting up to the eaves, could make out two or three large, black insects flying around the supporting roof timbers. It was all very well to minister to his every need, but it was time, he thought, to establish some financial ground rules.

"Est le prix?" he asked the pest control expert who was stepping into a disposable white boiler suit with hood and dust mask and pulling on latex protective gloves.

"Ah, ha ha," laughed M. Acrylic Jumper a little alarmingly. *"Pas cher, pas de tout cher, Monsieur. N'inquietez-vous pas!"* Being told it would not be expensive was not entirely reassuring.

The side-kick took the cue and was loading an evil-looking can – a can covered in government health warnings, yellow stickers bearing images of skull and crossbones – into some kind of electric pump. The window-cleaner was busily hoisting up a ladder and defeated, Starr went into the kitchen to make them all some good, strong coffee.

With the shouting and crashing outside, he didn't hear the arrival of his third visitor of the morning. There was no pre-warning of his presence and the first Starr knew was the smell of his breath next to him as he bent over his percolator. "Agh!" he cried out in genuine shock.

"*Excusez-moi*," laughed Dacour. "I had no intention of frightening you. Maybe you have a bad conscience?"

"What? No, no. You made me jump, that's all. I've got these guys getting rid of a hornets' nest in my roof," he waved vaguely in the direction of the door. "I'm glad to see you."

Dacour was, as usual, unhealthy and slightly crumpled-looking. With his dishevelled hair and his battered faux-leather jacket, creased at the back, he gave the impression of having slept in his car. For all Starr knew, he had. Dacour loaded the fresh cafetière of coffee, mugs and sugar onto a tray and before Starr could intercept him, was taking them out onto the bright but chilly terrace.

"You are lucky it is just hornets," he said. "Termites and *capricornes* are eating away whole streets in villages along the Dordogne," he continued merrily. "Even some of the chateaux are infested. I saw a van up at Chateau Benedictus last time I was there, treating the chai's charpente."

"Mmm beams," muttered Starr distractedly.

"I hope I am not inconveniencing you. I think we started out on the left foot."

Starr frowned. "Oh yes – the wrong foot, yes perhaps," he conceded.

"I am going to Paris tomorrow," the detective said. "Mademoiselle Janneau's apartment in the rue Clichy has been untouched and we have a police guard there now," he continued, offering Starr a Marboro before lighting both cigarettes, cupping his Bic lighter with his left hand against the morning breeze.

"Are you any nearer, Inspector, to knowing who might have, you know, done this?" Starr hated the way he was speaking in clichés but couldn't stop himself. His life since Sylvie's murder had begun to feel like a bad movie in which he was the character with the worst lines.

"Please, call me Erik."

"Oh OK," said Starr a little surprised. "Call me Franklin, then. Or Starr – as everyone round here does."

"You can be my *étoile*, my guiding star," the detective smiled the smile of a man unused to flexing his smile muscles. "I was hoping that perhaps you might have some ideas as to anyone who might wish Mademoiselle Janneau harm – a lover perhaps?"

Starr felt suspicious of the detective's sudden change of approach. From early antagonism, he was bending over backwards to be convivial and Starr had yet to understand the reason for the shift.

He didn't know how much the detective already knew of Sylvie's life, but thought he must know about the relationship with de Cazaux's wife, since Agnès would have told him during the second police interview.

"I didn't know her well," he said. "In fact I have only seen her a few times since she was a child. Her mother mentioned she was having a relationship with someone married," Starr managed to dodge specifying the gender of the adulterer.

"Mmm, yes. Madame de Cazaux," Dacour looked up and fixed Starr in a long enquiring stare as if to record the finest wavelengths of a reaction. "You met with Monsieur de Cazaux, I believe."

"Who? Oh sure. He wanted to pay his respects to Agnès, to Madame Janneau."

"You don't like him, Starr?"

"I don't know him. He appears to me to be very sophisticated, very privileged, super confident. He wears the right clothes and has the right manners."

"*L'habit ne fait pas le moine*," interjected Dacour.

"No sure – you can't judge a book by its cover. But he expects people to do what he says and I imagine he is rarely disappointed. He seemed sorry about Sylvie's death, but how do you judge? He did say something interesting. He says he had a text from her mentioning her meeting with Damien Refeuille, you remember I told you, and the Romanée-Conti '45."

"Do you know when it was sent? Did you see the message?"

"No that was a little odd. He said it was sent to his other cellphone; one he had left in Paris. I guess it would be on Sylvie's cellphone too."

Starr wanted to raise the issue of the phone without landing Christiane in it. However Dacour adroitly ducked the bait and instead wrote something in neat, small handwriting in his police notebook.

"He has motive: I cannot imagine many men to be happy that their wife is sleeping with an employee, even a woman. And he was here."

Starr noted the rather French attitude to adultery – all the less grave to be cuckolded by a woman.

"Yes. Did he have an alibi for Thursday night?" Starr wasn't sure of the etiquette of talking about a case with the leading investigator, but Dacour seemed eager to chat.

"Up until midnight, yes. He hosted a dinner for some negoçiants and wine-growers at the Plaisance. The hotel records show he signed for the meal at 11.45pm and then went up to his room. The reception desk confirmed he asked for a wake-up call on Friday morning at 7.30am and answered the phone. The desk is manned 24/7 and no-one saw Monsieur de Cazaux leave. He would have to have somehow climbed out of his bedroom window on the third floor and I have looked at the wall outside. There are no ledges or supports, no signs of disturbance. Honestly, I think it impossible, Monsieur, unless he crept past the reception desk unseen, and I cannot see Monsieur de Cazaux creeping, can you?"

"So what are you thinking?"

"I am not sure. The murder was planned. In *crimes passionels* strangling, stabbing or – how do you say? *coup de matraque* – is much more normal."

Dacour mimed each murder method all-too-realistically including the last – bludgeoning.

"This appears to have been done in cold blood," he continued. "The hotel stationery would have to have been found before forging the suicide note. The handwriting was perfect. Our expert confirmed it and even Monsieur Le Blond admitted it was a professional job. So someone planned the murder, knowing Sylvie would be in Saint-Emilion on Thursday night. But who and why? These are the questions. Did you know, Madame de Cazaux was also in Saint-Emilion last week?"

The piercing eyes of the detective burned with a curiosity intensified by the deathly, damp pallor of his face. Starr found it disquieting to the point where he could feel the palms of his hands growing slightly sweaty. It was as if Dacour could see every crime and misdemeanour ever committed by Starr; crimes of which Starr himself was ignorant. "I had no idea. But she wasn't staying with her husband?"

"No, not at la Plaisance. It appears she has an old school friend at Chateau Beauséjour and came down *sur un coup de tête.*"

"On a whim, I see," said Starr more and more intrigued.

"You may know this person. She has made quite a name for the wine there. She is Cappucine Montélimar."

"Oh really? Everyone knows the name. What's she's done with that old vineyard is nothing short of magic."

Starr had never met Cappucine Montélimar but she was a towering legend even in the fairytale world of Bordeaux wine-making. He didn't know a great deal about her: only that she had bought up an almost abandoned small vineyard just on the southern borders of Saint-Emilion with a crumbling house and derelict chai, and had systematically restored all three to the point where now Beauséjour had become highly collectable. The tiny vineyard only produced about 8,000 bottles in a vintage putting it almost in the *garagiste*class. She was the recipient of many awards and remarkable partly due to her gender in a landscape still very much dominated by men.

"Have you spoken to Madame de Cazaux?"

"Not so far, no. She has returned to Paris and I have a *rendez-vous* with her arranged for after the weekend. Madame Montélimar has confirmed her alibi though. They were both together the whole of the evening of last Thursday, the night of Sylvie's death. They are each other's alibis."

The French detective took a long, thoughtful mouthful of black coffee and moving his head from side to side simply said,

"There are many players in this *drame*. I think there is more to this young woman's life than we know so far. With no witnesses, no DNA on the body, we have to hope the murderer was careless, made an error. In all my time as a *flic* it is not the cleverness of the police but the stupidity of the criminal that in the end brings justice."

Starr poured them both refills from his cooling coffee jug and asked,

"If there's anything I can help with, you must say. I am a bit of an outsider here, but..." he trailed off.

"You are a little bit an insider and an outsider, and that is why I think you can help us with this challenging crime. There may be things you think of, or hear. Here is my card with my *numéro portable*. You can call me anytime. We have assigned a detective to work with me – a female gendarme on temporary secondment here. She has trained in criminal psychology and will, I hope, compensate for my pedestrian, male logic," his lined face broke into another unnatural smile and he got up to leave. "Until the cuts, our brigade had six detectives," he continued. "Now we have to do the same work with half the resource."

As they made their way to the car, the pest controller was stuffing his disposable boiler suit and gloves into Starr's wheelie-bin and the acrylic jumper was fixing his ladder back onto the roof of his 2CV van.

The engine of his unmarked grey metallic diesel Peugeot 405 growling loudly, Dacour wound down the window and Starr just made out "Christiane Montreux," as he reversed into the lane.

The hornets dealt with, peace returned to La Borie. Even in a week the first green tendrils on the vines were now sprouting into vigorous life. Each day the sun shone a little warmer and longer as March turned into April and the individual chateau tastings gave way to the more business-like group tastings. These were where press and négociant reactions to the vintage would trickle into the eventual release price. The producers only set the price after they had got feedback and initial orders. It was a secretive and arcane system with its challengers but it nevertheless dominated the sale of the vast majority of the finest Bordeaux chateaux. Chateaux owners got the advantage of positive cashflow and shrewd buyers could make tidy profits. Anyone, thought Starr, a little bitterly since he wasn't one of them, who'd bought a case of Pétrus 2005 in the en primeur season in 2007 would have paid no more than €12,000. A few weeks later cases were changing hands at €22,000. By 2012 you'd have needed over €38,000 for the same wine.

Starr was always invited along to the main bun fights, even though God knows, he was only a small investor in en primeur. His wife Esmé said they liked his American lack of polish. "You're the grit, Frank," (she was the only one ever to call him Frank and get away with it). "They love your uncouth, American roughness. It's what these events need: some grit in the oyster."

Usually he didn't go. He made an exception for the Chateau Benedictus party, partly because de Bachelet had been consistently charming, welcoming when he and Esmé were killing themselves restoring La Borie each summer, and partly, well, even before Benedictus had been promoted to *grand cru classé* status he knew class when he drank it. Benedictus had class, but did it have form, his mind wandered vaguely.

Quite different motivations underlay his acceptance of the invitation to the Cercle Rive Droite tastings that afternoon. The Cercle included over 140 chateaux from 19 appelations stretching all along the river from Sainte Foy in the east to Montagne Saint-Emilion and Lussac in the west. It included some of the most illustrious and expensive wines of the right bank.

With a flash of inspiration he found Dacour's card and dialled his cellphone. The inspector gave him Christiane Montreux's number without hesitation. She'd agreed to come along "in disguise" so they could observe the wine aristocracy at its most showy without arousing suspicion.

"Remember no perfume," he thought it wise to advise.

"I am not a barbarian, Monsieur. I may not be a Girondine but that doesn't mean I wasn't *bien elevée*," she said, as if wearing perfume, deodorant or after-shave to a wine-tasting was as obvious a social gaffe as spitting on the floor.

As he dressed in his one blue suit, he paid slightly more attention than usual to how he looked. The appearance of Dacour made him keen to disassociate himself from that particular brand of the untended, middle-aged male. He shaved carefully and found matching socks.

He arrived at the address she'd given him in Libourne a good 20 minutes early. Why had Madame de Cazaux stayed with Cappucine Montélimar rather than at the hotel Plaisance with her husband? He was trying to knit together the strands of the story, to understand a pattern, when there was a tap on the window.

Christiane Montreux was transformed since the two had shared a watery tea in a gloomy café in Libourne. She was wearing a jade green, fitted dress made from some kind of drapey, stretchy fabric and heels. Her jet black short bobbed hair shone in the afternoon sun and the bright red lipstick accentuated her generous mouth. Starr tried to guess her age, but found it difficult. She was certainly out of her twenties, but she could have been anything between 33 and 45, he thought.

"Sorry, I'm waiting for Christiane Montreux," Starr tried a harmless joke.

"Ha, ha," she said, sliding into the seat beside him. She fumbled in her handbag and put on some outsize Jackie-O style sunglasses.

The Chateau Grand Barrail, now a hotel, was the epitome of the popular cliché of the archetypal French chateau. It commanded the surrounding parkland and vineyards in maximalist 19th century splendour; its pale cream stone walls rising to meet majestic corner turrets, its complicated roof capped with metallic grey slate. The whole, grand edifice was surrounded by broad gravel terraces, each bordered by a low stone ballustrade. In reality the Grand Barrail resembled few of the great chateaux, especially those in Saint-Emilion, most of which were plain, surprisingly modest square-built old houses with terracotta Roman tile roofs.

The lack of understatement extended to the car park. Here gleaming in the sun were the latest models of Range Rover, BMW, Mercedes, Maserati, Ferrari, Lamborghini – not a humble domestic car to be seen. Starr steered the battered old Peugeot 605 alongside a Porsche 911 convertible he thought he recognised.

"It's worse than Saint Tropez," said Christiane. "I've never seen such a collection of cars. There must be millions of euros just here in the parking!" Something about her girlish naivety struck Starr as forced – she was giving him a performance.

"This is nothing. The Cercle Rive Droite is the most important event of the en primeur campaign except for the UGC tastings in Bordeaux. All the money will be here. But I guess you knew that, right?" Starr said as they joined the throng crunching their way over the deep gravel to the tall double doors of the hotel's front lobby. The police-woman didn't answer but looked away.

"Is there anything specific you want me to look out for – or anyone you would like me to introduce you to?" Starr asked, keeping his voice low.

"Clearly I am curious to see Damien Refeuille, but I want to observe him. It is vital he does not see me, that I not meet him," said Christiane forcefully. "We don't know if Gilles de Cazaux is still here?" the upward inflection of what would otherwise be a statement tipping it into the interrogative.

Starr thought back to his meeting with de Cazaux at the Hostellerie de Plaisance earlier in the week. "I think he was planning to go back to Paris, but that was before the Procureur made the announcement about the murder investigation. If I see him, shall I point him out?"

"Yes please. I am particularly interested to see Monsieur de Cazaux."

They were now inside the chateau in its grand marble entrance hall, flanked on three sides by floor-to-ceiling windows that showed off the fabulous views of vineyards and distant copses, like a southern version of an 18th century English landscape painting. Starr nudged Christiane and pointed to the enormous crystal chandelier that seemed to float like a spaceship designed by Swarovski in the air above them.

The room was filled with chatter and anticipation as they were funnelled down a wide passageway flanked by repro bronze-effect statues to the grand salon beyond. Here narrow trestles, covered to the floor with white linen cloths, had been arranged around the entire perimeter of the stately room. Banners bearing the Cercle Rive Droite logo in Bordeaux wine and gold hung from the ceiling and a photographer was busily snapping a small, bespectacled Chinese guy Starr thought might have been de Bachelet's air conditioning billionaire now being courted by the *caviste* of one of Saint-Emilion's starriest chateaux.

Starr was scanning the room for Gilles de Cazaux when a tall, distinguished figure tapped him on the shoulder.

"Ah Monsieur de Bachelet," Starr greeted the aristocratic wine-grower. "Checking out the competition?"

"Alas, Monsieur. You Americans are obsessed with the marketplace. For me this is like visiting the Louvre. A single gallery: a hundred works of art." His eyebrows lifted slightly in enquiry as he saw Christiane at Starr's side.

"Let me introduce Christiane Montreux," said Starr. "She is new to the region and something of an oenophile."

The towering de Bachelet bent his head and taking Christiane's hand kissed it in the old-fashioned way. "*Enchanté Madame*," he said, eyes twinkling. "You must persuade Monsieur Starr to bring you to my little vineyard. I would be delighted to show you our chai."

Christiane smiled in agreement.

"I have just been talking to the wine editor of *Cuvée* magazine, Monsieur Charpentier. He thinks this may be a great year for the right bank."

Starr listened intently and noticed that Christiane was too.

"You know Monsieur Charpentier?" Starr asked.

"Everyone knows Valentin Charpentier, Starr. He is the greatest wine writer in the world," and with that Guy de Bachelet bowed slightly and was caught up in new conversations with yet more négociants.

Starr steered Christiane Montreux away deeper into the melée and towards Chateau Gaby's spot. "Try this," he encouraged her. "It's one of my favourites."

Starr was just allowing the young rough wine to develop in his mouth, its tannins still overpowering the underlying fruit, when a forceful wallop on his back nearly made him choke.

"You're such a predictable sod, Starr. There's more to Saint-Emilion than Gaby you know," Shawcross was filled with the good humour of a major buyer securing his allocations.

"Jim, do me a favour. Can you introduce me to that négociant, Refeuille? I'm sure he's here."

Shawcross turned on Starr, almost aggressively.

"What the hell do you want with that bottom feeder? If you want a deal, just tell me what you're after. I can get you in front of a decent seller. You don't want to touch that piece of slime from the bottom of the pond. Honestly."

This was perhaps the longest speech Starr had ever witnessed from Shawcross and his emotion was palpable. He didn't have time to find out what lay behind his old friend's animosity, but he did need his co-operation.

"For Christ's sake, I'm not interested in buying from him, you meathead," said Starr. "Listen it's to do with Sylvie's murder. I just need you to introduce us, that's all."

Shawcross looked long and hard at Starr. "Have you done something? Had a haircut? You look, sort of, different."

"Stop changing the subject. Please," Starr pleaded.

Shawcross was not one to jump or indeed make any quick movements, but he did wade with surprising speed in his usual, blundering style to the corner of the grand room where Refeuille was to be found lurking.

"Hello there. It's Monsieur Refeuille isn't it?" Shawcross was struggling to sound civil. "Jim Shawcross, Williams & Williams."

Refeuille passed a tanned hand through his long, floppy hair before offering it to the untidy Englishman. "I know who you are."

"Oh good. Well I wanted to introduce a friend of mine, lives in the area and buys a bit, you know both en primeur and at auction. Anyway I'll leave you two to it," and he was gone, diving into the throng, his unruly hair surfacing occasionally like a dolphin's dorsal fin in a rough sea.

"Franklin Starr, *enchanté*." Starr hadn't prepared what he was going to say and wanted to play for time to ensure Christiane had taken up a position at an adjoining table, safely two or three people away, but within earshot and sight of the négociant.

"Are you looking for something in particular?" Refeuille was undoubtedly charming, thought Starr.

"Well as a matter of fact I am. I'm planning a birthday party. A real special birthday party and I was hoping to find some outstanding vintages for it. Only trouble is, they're not wines readily available. Shawcross said you are a bit of an expert in sourcing rarities," said Starr, hoping he sounded believable.

"Ah. Rarities. Rarities are by definition hard to find, Monsieur. And of course the rarer the wine, the higher the price. Did you have any specific rarities in mind?" Refeuille smiled encouragingly.

Starr thought quickly. "Budget's no issue," he said, getting out his notebook and pretending to read a list. He was anxious to appear ignorant, not to put Refeuille on his guard. "I'm looking for a Cheval Blanc '47 and err a Pétrus – is that how you pronounce it? – 1961, for example. Someone back home recommended them."

"These are not easy wines to come by, Monsieur," said Refeuille. "But fortunately you have come to the right place. I am something of an expert in sourcing very rare premier cru wines of the region, and also have a special private collection that I have built up over the years. Perhaps I can invite you to my office here in Saint-Emilion? I would be delighted to show you round any time next week after the en primeur season."

"That would be great," said Starr, feeling about in his inside coat pocket for a card he had once had printed. "Here are my details."

Starr wasn't quite sure how the card had somehow dropped between them, but it did. As Refeuille bent down to pick it up, a mobile phone with a purple clip-on case dropped out of his left coat pocket. He picked it up and looked at it for a few seconds.

"Not your phone?" asked Starr intrigued.

Refeuille hesitated but before he could decide what to do, Christiane was there, pulling her badge from her handbag.

"Give me the handset, Monsieur," she ordered, and holding out a clean handkerchief, wrapped it up and put it in her handbag.

"I don't know how that phone got into my coat. It's nothing to do with me," remonstrated Refeuille. Starr caught the briefest look of recognition in Refeuille's brown eyes, as Christiane dealt with him.

"We will have plenty of time to discuss it later," said the detective. "It may be nothing, but it may be a piece of critical evidence. You will come with me now to the police station while we verify its owner."

"But..." said Refeuille. "I can't come now. It's the Cercle Rive Droite. I don't understand. What are you doing? It's just a phone."

"I suggest you come immediately so we do not have to cause any unnecessary publicity," said Christiane and she firmly pushed Refeuille in front of her and nodded for Starr to follow.

CHAPTER

6

Dacour was no doubt congratulating himself that he had the full club quatre area to himself on the morning TGV to Paris Montparnasse. He had spread out his papers, his laptop, plugged into the socket under the table, his battered briefcase and the fake leather jacket he was never without.

Starr paused, unseen for a few minutes, to watch him. He was a grey, disappointed man. He looked drawn, tired and faintly troubled. His vinyl briefcase bulged with paperwork, his clothes no longer quite fitted him and the dark circles under his eyes and the pallor of his face were the marks of an insomniac. He gave the impression of a man who has long given up. There was an intensity in his eyes accentuated by the listlessness of the rest of him. They were the colour of the vast tidal bore of the Gironde, the Mascaret, at its spring height: a matte grey that bears the memory of blue somewhere in its recessive depths.

He pulled from his briefcase a magazine, *La Dixième Muse*, with the image of a tousled-haired young woman on its cover. Starr couldn't help but admire the style with which he opened France's most-read lesbian magazine, with as much insouciance as if he were checking out the sports pages of the *Sud-Ouest*. Now and then he circled a passage or advertisement with a blue felt tip pen.

Dacour was not behaving like a detective who has his prime suspect snared and securely held in a police cell, thought Starr. What Dacour was actually thinking of Refeuille was hidden behind the detective's habitual frown: a series of ripples that gave his forehead the appearance of a section of Arcachon beach that the outgoing tide has moulded by its eddying forces.

The phone in his inside jacket pocket vibrated. He glanced at the number before answering,

"*Christiane, je t'écoute.*" A long conversation followed with Dacour simply grunting in response.

"*Bien, Christiane,*" says Dacour. "Hold Monsieur Refeuille. We don't have to charge him for 48 hours. Let him smoke and have coffee and water, *un sandwich*. I don't want anyone talking to him until I'm back. *Compris?*"

"His *avocat* is Maitre Brune?" Dacour whistled loudly.

"*Vraiment?* Then Monsieur Refeuille has both powerful connections and deep pockets. Inform the Bordeaux office of Maitre Brune that we are waiting for forensics to finish their report on the victim's phone found in his client's possession before questioning him. We are not charging him at this time. That should keep him off our back for a day or two."

He hung up and the ripples on his brow deepened into narrower contours, like a steep escarpment on a topographic map.

By the time Starr swung his lanky frame into the seat opposite him, Dacour was dozing fitfully, his head lolling against the window of the speeding train. Starr noted the magazine with its blue pen annotations, the briefcase bulging untidily, the detective's habitual pallor.

Flipping off the plastic lid, Starr quietly sipped his macchiato and gazed at the smudged green landscape apparently accelerating past them, like a tourist film on steroids. He'd almost been taken in by Dacour's feint. But some false note sounded in the detective's phone call claiming he had postponed his trip to Paris, he couldn't identify what. Starr smiled. It was always a pleasure to be proved right.

The train took a curve sharply to the left bumping Dacour's head and waking him up. Seeing Starr opposite him, he merely frowned.

"Would you like a coffee?" asked Starr brightly.

"Hmm. Double espresso. *Merci.*"

The TGV's café-bar was only a carriage away and Starr was back within a few minutes.

"So," he said as he manoeuvred himself into the seat opposite the crumpled detective, "Change of plan?"

Dacour merely grunted in reply and tore off the end of the sugar and poured it carefully into his steaming espresso.

"Visiting a relative perhaps? Catching an exhibition?" he was pushing his luck, he knew, but Starr felt buoyed with confidence.

The detective hunched his shoulders and spread out his tanned hands in front of him in reply. "It was a last-minute decision," he lied.

"I'm intrigued. You clearly don't think Refeuille did it," said Starr, diving in.

"It is far too early to say what part, if any, Monsieur Refeuille played in this affair. It looks bad for him, that I believe. But I do not yet have a clear picture of Sylvie Janneau and her life. I am going to Paris to try to change that position, as much as to question possible suspects."

"Are you going to see Madame de Cazaux?"

Dacour looked hard at Starr, the murky grey eyes boring into him, before he tilted his head and very faintly nodded.

"Is there any chance I could come along, maybe as an advisor, or I don't know, in some capacity? She's never met me so there's no chance of recognition."

"That would be irregular, Starr. You know that," and closed the subject.

Starr got up and went through the automatic doors of the carriage into the little corridor where two other passengers were also making calls. He dialled Agnès' cellphone and told her he was on the train and wanted to meet Marie-Joëlle de Cazaux.

"Leave it with me," Agnès replied. "You will stay tonight, yes?" she continued. "I will book a table – would you like to try Thoumieux?"

Starr had never eaten at the Left-Bank brasserie taken over by the head chef of the super-glamorous Hotel de Crillon but it had been on his list for a year now. Quite apart from the food, which would be revelatory he felt sure, he wanted to see for himself the Vegas-inspired decor put together by the hip Paris designer, India Mahdavi.

"Are you kidding!" he said enthusiastically.

"I'll text you with a message about Madame de Cazaux, OK?" Agnès rang off and Starr returned to his spot opposite Dacour.

"You are very transparent, Starr," he said.

"Yeh? Well that's probably because I'm a simple American and don't have your European layers."

"Not so simple, I think," Dacour's face was poker straight.

"Tell me, why are you OK with discussing the case now, when you were so hostile to me just a day or two ago?"

"I am never hostile," said the detective. "But it is true that my first impression was of a close family friend letting his emotions get in the way of reason."

"And now?"

"And now, I am prepared to concede that your, how do you say, 'unch about the suicide note was right. Maybe you will have other 'unches that can help us. With over 100 suspects already, we can certainly benefit from some amateur help," he said, emphasising the 'amateur'.

"I am at your disposal, and as keen to nail the guy as you. Out there in the vineyards there's a killer. He must be found."

Dacour looked at the American quizzically and after a long pause, said, "Or she."

Starr arrived in the rue Saint-Dominique in Paris' 7th arrondissement early. The faded 1930s neon sign that hung outside the restaurant was an early indicator of the unpretentiousness and the playfulness that lay within. He decided to go straight up to the brasserie on the first floor and enjoy a drink at the bar while he waited for Agnès.

There was already an inviting buzz in this paean to 'more is more' design. The mass of mirrored glass columns, opaque globe lamps and dark red banquettes fused a neo-Baroque style with the bling of a Bollywood set. Starr loved it. He settled on a tall bar chair with a good view in the mirror behind of the entrance so he wouldn't miss Agnès and ordered a Grey Goose and tonic. It was rare for him to drink spirits, not because of some religious devotion to his palate – the cigarettes had long put paid to that – but because in the corner of the Médoc where he lived, wine was all and it was unthinkable to drink anything else.

Starr studied the reflections of the clientèle – a jostling mix of hip Parisians and international visitors from a party of guys in their 20s to an elegant couple well in their 70s. This was modern Paris, where the old social tramlines that once dictated life's journey and its stops, no longer existed, or if they did, no longer ran on predictable routes.

Thoumieux's great chef, Jean-François Piège, had managed to earn two Michelin stars for this eatery by reinventing classics of French brasserie cuisine. The medal could be a drawback, five letters, thought Starr, his mind back to turning clues, like an old slot machine. Award. But he didn't have time for more useless wordplay because here was Agnès, smoothing back her blonde hair and slipping out of her coat. Starr rose to greet her and they were shown to their table.

As Agnès deftly put on her reading glasses, Starr was again struck by her natural attractiveness: an easy beauty, liveable with, he thought. She chose the *velouté de crustaces* to start while he the *paté de foie de volaille de ma mère* as the menu described it, lending the dish that sense of intimacy and neighbourhood that the swathes of Parisian brasseries now owned and managed by huge chains so completely lacked. They both decided on the entrecôte with béarnaise sauce and matchstick fries – *allumettes*.

Starr decided to push the boat out and ordered a 2005 Chateau Ausone to drink with their steak and they each started with a glass of white wine – she a *Muscadet* and he a small Sauternes whose sweetness would bring out the round, fat flavours of the liver paté perfectly.

After half an hour in the warm restaurant Starr at last stopped feeling cold for the first time since leaving the blossom-strewn platform of Libourne. As he got up to take off his jacket and put it on the back of his chair, Agnès reached across the table and sotto voce, said,

"Jean-Francois Piège is a legend, you know. He trained under Alain Ducasse," as if telling him some very privileged secret, rather than the public knowledge to be found in any review on TripAdvisor.

"Yes, I know," said Starr. "What was the name of that chef you used to see?"

Agnès coloured slightly. "Thierry Malbec."

"That's right. Didn't you once have a thing, you two?"

Agnès nodded. "Once, well twice actually," she grinned.

"Agnès Janneau, I am shocked!"

They continued in this easy vein, their conversation illuminated by small pictures of the past until Agnès, just as she was starting on her rhum baba, frowned and became reflective.

"Franklin, do you think Monsieur Refeuille is Sylvie's killer?" she asked.

"I really don't know," Starr shook his head. "He had a motive. I think there is no doubt he is involved in some complex wine fraud and Sylvie found him out. That's for sure. According to the police he has no alibi for the time after he and Sylvie left the restaurant that night, so theoretically it's possible. But he strikes me as too weak to kill. Greedy and immoral, sure, but a killer? What I will say Agnès, is he seemed genuinely surprised when that phone fell out of his pocket. Either he's a very good actor or he'd not seen it before."

"You think it's de Cazaux, don't you?"

"I don't know, but put it this way. I can more easily accept Gilles de Cazaux would have the mental strength to plan and carry out a killing than Refeuille. I am intensely curious to meet the wife – Madame de Cazaux."

"She will charm even you," smiled Agnès.

Starr was already convinced he would not take to this privileged, manipulative woman.

"We'll see about that."

The rue Maspéro in the one-time village of Passy in Paris' upmarket 16th arrondissement was a short walk from the metro station at Muette.

As Starr took Agnès' arm, he became acutely conscious of the sound of his shoes on the pavement and remembered reading somewhere that

Eric Satie attributed all the rhythms of his music to the sounds of his footsteps as he walked the streets of Paris.

"I don't really know the 16th," Starr said as much to himself as to his companion.

"The discreet charm of the 16th," laughed Agnès.

"Is it still kind of upper class?"

"Passy is still full of old families with old money, yes. And of course the bobo set."

"Who are they?"

"Oh you know. Bourgeois – so well off, well-educated, good family, but also Bohemian, a little *marginale*," explained Agnès. "You will find the *gauche-caviar* here."

"What are *they*?" Starr hadn't come across the phrase.

"Socialists, leftish intellectuals with money. It's very expensive to live here, you know."

Starr looked up at the elegant 19th century buildings with their large wooden entrances and rococo, frivolous wrought iron balconies.

"You of all people should love Passy," continued Agnès.

"Why's that?"

"This is where your namesake, Benjamin Franklin, lived, almost up to the Revolution in 1785. He was very popular in Paris – perhaps there's never been an American Paris has taken more to their hearts."

"Who else lived here?"

"Oh lots of people, but perhaps none so famous as Balzac. You know he lived under a false name and chose a house with a back exit into a different street so he could easily escape when his creditors came for him."

"So it's true then that he really was in debt all his life, in spite of *La Comédie Humaine*."

"Or perhaps because of it," said Agnès. "Here we are!"

As they found the buzzer with the name 'de Cazaux' in black copperplate next to it, the small door cut into the building's entrance buzzed open and they stepped into a beautiful, private courtyard, stone-flagged with large terracotta pots from which were sprouting the glossy foliage of orange trees. On the right were an open entrance, a sweeping shallow stone staircase and a lift.

A cloud of Agnès's scent mixed with the smell of polished mahogany gave Starr a slightly erotic thrill as the tiny wooden box ascended to the fifth floor. He couldn't remember when he had been so filled with anticipation at meeting someone – *la femelle d'espece* –the female of the species.

The door to the de Cazaux family apartment was opened by a comfortable-looking, middle-aged woman. Starr spent perhaps two seconds trying to fit his preconceptions about Madame de Cazaux to the figure in front of them before realising she was some kind of retainer.

"Madame is expecting you," she said in French and took their coats and Agnès' umbrella that she was never without, before opening a large double door into an enormous, light-flooded reception room. The chalky white walls were hung with a mix of old and contemporary art in exquisite taste, the original plaster mouldings of the ceilings adding interest but not over-elaboration, here and there were beautiful examples of antique French furniture while at one end an enormous, contemporary sofa in powder-blue invited informal lounging.

Facing them with her back to the floor to ceiling windows and as a result with her face in shadow was Madame de Cazaux. She didn't speak.

"Do you have any objection if I sit on the sofa?" asked Starr.

"I have no objection to anything, Monsieur," replied the apartment's chatelaine, her voice deep and sensual.

She then rose and greeted Agnès by kissing her three times on alternate cheeks in the usual manner.

"Agnès – such a pleasure to see you."

Madame de Cazaux was not tall, petite even, with shoulder length brown hair, dressed in impeccably cut narrow trousers, flat ballet pumps and a silk blouse with a cardigan balancing on her shoulders. Starr noted the large diamond engagement ring and simple wedding band, a vintage Patek Philippe Tank on her wrist. Probably 1940s, judging by the plain, oblong face and blue crocodile strap, thought Starr, enviously, because he'd always wanted a Patek.

"Céline," Madame de Cazaux raised her hand in a half wave to the woman who had answered the door and lurked at the far end of the enormous room.

"I thought we should have a small *coupe, n'est ce pas?*" she addressed Agnès exclusively. It was as if Starr wasn't there. The anonymity suited him fine – it allowed him to take in every detail without appearing rude. He clocked her tiny, elegant ankles, her small, tapering fingers, but most of all he noticed her eyes. They were very large, almond-shaped, heavy-lidded and in a striking shade of green, not olive, but vivid green. Her face was beautiful – there really was no other word for it – in that classic sense that comes from excellent bone structure and strong, symmetrical features. Her beauty was of the long life kind: there was no sell-by date. It would go with her to the grave. She must be two decades older than poor Sylvie, he guessed, and quite a few years older than her husband too but seductive, fascinating, complex.

It was then that Starr noticed a small loom in the corner of the room from which hung a mane of multi-coloured threads. A work was clearly in progress.

"Do you weave, Madame?" Starr turned to address his hostess.

"Don't we all?" she answered enigmatically. "I understand you are fond of puzzles, yes? You make word webs to trap your prey, no?"

Starr felt curiously uncomfortable and irritated that he was losing control of the conversation. And yet he was unaccountably keen to impress her.

"I have always believed you get closer to the truth by pretending not to speak it," he tried a little philosophy.

"Ah *la verité*. A lie travels round the world while the truth is putting her boots on. You are familiar, *sans doute*, with the expression, Monsieur Starr?"

"Yes indeed. And of course another great French aphorism – half the truth is often a whole lie."

A coldness had entered the room – an atmosphere of suspicion and almost malice. It was Agnès who sought to rescue them all from its grip.

"This is such a lovely apartement, Marie-Joëlle. Have you lived here long?"

"Thank you, Agnès. I'm not sure I would have chosen the 16th, but it is convenient for Gilles' office and he is very at home here in Passy. For me, it's like Garrison Keillor says, full of good people in the worst sense of the word," she smiled at Starr, like an opponent who has just declared 'check'.

Céline arrived with a glass and silver tray bearing a bottle of Dom Perignon in a cooler and three crystal glasses. The champagne had been opened and she carefully poured each flute with no more than half a glass of the cold, straw-coloured wine.

"*Santé*," said Madame de Cazaux raising her glass first to Agnès and then to Starr. They each took a virginal sip.

"I expect you want to ask me about my relationship with Sylvie," she addressed Starr, who nearly choked. "We were lovers."

"Err," Starr found himself stumbling around in verbal darkness, suddenly lost for words.

"Have I robbed you of the power of speech?" she asked raising one perfectly-arched eyebrow. "The policeman from Libourne was the same. So very tongue-tied," she continued. "While you compose yourself, I will tell you a little about it. We met at some very tedious book launch of Gilles' exactly two and a half years ago. It was instant, the attraction between us, and we were physical lovers within days of meeting. Sylvie was an extraordinary woman. Beautiful of course, but very refined, very discerning. She had a huge appetite to discover the world, and for me, I adored being able to share some of my personal discoveries with her. We were passionately, wholly in love. She took me to clubs in the Marais, you know, where we danced to techno and I took her to Marrakech, to the Jardins Majorelle and the Atlas mountains. We discovered each other's unknown territories like 16th century explorers. We were Columbus and de Gama setting sail without maps, without fear."

"What about your marriage, your husband?" interjected Starr.

"Oh really, Monsieur Starr. I didn't think you were so provincial. Gilles and I have been married for 15 years and are utterly devoted to each other and our beautiful twins. He has his *maîtresses* and I my own objects of passion. We are not in America here."

"Did Sylvie understand that too or was she provincial?"

"Sylvie could never be provincial. She was far too original and free. We lived in the now, in the moment. There was no past and no future when we were together. Just an intense experiencing of the present."

"You must have been devastated by news of her...death."

"Devastated is too small a word, Monsieur Starr. I was – I am – undone. The loss is unbearable."

Starr noticed that Madame de Cazaux's eyes were swimming in tears that brimmed but never fell.

"Do you have any idea, any suspicion, of who might be responsible?" asked Starr.

"If I had the faintest suspicion, that person would not be breathing," Madame de Cazaux recovered herself and took a bigger sip of the Champagne.

"You know the police are holding a negociant, Damien Refeuille, who had her mobile phone."

"I am aware of that, yes. Of course I know Monsieur Refeuille by reputation – not personally. I have a very old friend, Cappucine Montélimar, who is a winemaker in the region. You may know her perhaps? She says he is despicable, a complete crook. I hope they have the right man, Monsieur."

And with that, Agnès and Starr were under no illusion the audience was at an end and they all rose to bid goodbye.

Starr was about to follow Agnès out into the landing in front of the lift when Madame de Cazaux gripped his hand. Looking up into his eyes she said urgently, "Do not judge me, Monsieur."

CHAPTER

7

S tarr stretched a foot from under the bedcovers to the curtains of his bedroom window and gave them a good yank. Without moving from the cosy warmth of his bed he could drink in the view that had first seduced him over 15 years ago. The early morning sun was already warm and the pale haze of the horizon was fast melting into the fine azure sky above. Beyond the low stone walls of his terraced gardens, where deep blue irises – the original fleur-de-lis – caught the breeze, was an undulating landscape of nothing but vines stretching in every direction. The blackened stumps were now sprouting vigorously, the vivid green of the new leaves glowing like alien embers in the still-low sun. The tall trachycarpus palm that grew next to the house was, he saw, covered with the light green folded fans of new growth. The wisteria along his barn was in full bloom, its long mauve tails of flowers dancing along the old stone walls, and several little brown wall lizards were already stretched out sunbathing. Just like Donald Sutherland in *Kelly's Heroes*, thought Starr, "drinking wine, eating cheese and catching some rays." That pretty much summed up the sweet life.

Spring arrived in the Gironde in a rush, not politely with a few crocus here, an hour of sunlight there. Here you felt the life-force that had been pent up through the harsh, cold winter come crashing through the earth. Everything was growing, sprouting and opening and it was impossible not to feel the pulse quicken surrounded by all this fecundity.

He checked the local weather forecast on his iPhone and smiled at the round yellow sun and its prediction of a high of 26 degrees. Showered and shaved, Starr clattered down the old wooden staircase, picked up the *Sud-Ouest* that old Viremouneix always left on the kitchen table together with a baguette and if you were lucky a *chocolatine*, and started on his ritual coffee making routine.

He whistled the tune to Fats Waller's 'Honeysuckle Rose' as the sun streamed through the door to the garden where the smell of a warming earth mixed with the vanilla coffee that was percolating inside. Starr wiggled his toes in rhythm to his tune and drummed the side of the cafetière with a couple of teaspoons. It was over two decades since he'd played the bones in his student days at Harvard, but his passion for the music of Fats Waller, Tommy Dorsey, Artie Shaw and Chet Baker was unabated. The last time he'd actually practised his trombone was when the original five had got together for a reunion in New York's Café Carlyle. He'd never have been a Jack Teagarden that was for sure, but he'd been a passable, even witty slider. What strange alchemy had turned the original five big-haired members of Quince Jam (how pleased Starr had been with *that*, all those years ago) into two Wall Street traders, an eminent neuroscientist, a cynical attorney and a crossword-compiler for the *New York Times*?

Starr suddenly decided to dig out the old paperclip (as the French, *trombone* has it) from the loft. The hatch was stiff but eventually it gave way and the metal folding steps unbent to give him access. Fumbling about for the light switch, Starr squeezed his broad bony shoulders through the hole and was amazed by the sheer quantity of boxes, old bits of broken furniture and his parents' old leather suitcases that filled the huge roof space. The large trombone case was relatively easy to spot among the cityscape of towering cardboard, and with some awkward manoeuvering, Starr got it down.

He was attempting Mingus' 'Jelly Roll' out on the terrace, and doing a bad job it would be fair to say, when the familiar crunch of gravel announced a morning visitor.

"Bloody hell, Starr. You'll frighten the horses with that racket. What's going on?"

Shawcross was always a welcome visitor at La Borie and the already promising morning just got better with his appearance.

"Long story," replied Starr. "I'm surprised you're still here. I thought you'd be back in Mayfair, calculating your annual bonus by now!"

"Ah, well. I may be here for some weeks yet." Shawcross made a characteristic movement in which he slowly tilted his head from side to side. It usually meant he had bad news and was playing for time.

"Coffee?" suggested Starr, diving into the dark kitchen to make a fresh pot. He had started on the story of his meeting with Madame de Cazaux but his words were swallowed by the deafening noise of the coffee grinder, which stopped just as Shawcross yelled "What?" as though he was hailing a distant shepherd in a Force 9 gale on Edgecote Moor. Starr gave up and the two old friends walked to the terrace.

Since Shawcross showed no signs of saying what was on his chest, Starr said, "Come on then. Spill."

"Mmm. Something's been going on and I haven't been totally honest with you about it."

"What sort of something?"

"It's a nasty business, Franklin. Something that threatens the whole of the Bordeaux wine trade, its reputation, its chateaux, vignerons, négociants, auctioneers, you name it."

"Not *Flavescence Dorée*?" Starr was well aware of the growing vine disease that threatened to decimate the region's vineyards as much as Phylloxera had in the past.

"No it's not a disease, Franklin, at least not a natural disease. This is of human making."

"Go on, Jim."

"You know that Damien Refeuille. You thought he might have something to do with Sylvie's murder. Well, I think he's involved in something else. It all started last year when the DCF – you know, the French anti-fraud people – asked me to give an opinion of 17 cases of 1982 Pétrus that Sotheby's were auctioning in Hong Kong. They flew me out and three bottles were selected randomly for a careful tasting." Shawcross took a large gulp of his coffee.

"Isn't 1982 Pétrus the most faked wine in the world? What was the provenance?"

"Bang on, Starr. Just what I said. But the provenance was impeccable. Beyond the wine coming from the Pétrus cellars themselves the wine could not have had a better story. Anyway it was a fraught affair. There was the chief wine auctioneer from Sotheby's of course, a contingent of Mandarins from the Chinese AQSIQ and some French detective, a youngish bird, seconded from the anti-fraud police here. I had a pretty good look at the bottles, the labels and later the corks. The glass looked right. The labels too, so I was hoping the wine would match."

"*L'habit ne fait pas le moine,*" Starr quoted Dacour's remark. "It means you can't judge a book by its cover. The habit doesn't make the monk, literally."

"Aye, well, that's the truth. There were a dozen eyes on me. But I didn't have to taste it. From the moment they poured the wine into a glass I knew. This was no Pétrus, let alone one of their greatest vintages. All three bottles were fakes. Wine maybe five years old, no more. The tannins weren't fully integrated and it was a joke really. Wine that you could pick up at Leclerc for €4, being passed off as one of history's best examples of the art."

"So what then?"

"The wine was seized by the French and brought back to the lab in Pessac for proper testing."

"I've heard of that place."

"Apparently it leads the world. Quite extraordinary. They test radioactivity levels, the precise composition of the glass, the glue used to stick the labels, the levels of lead and nitrates, down to molecule level. The upshot was the glass was right, the labels were a mix of original and very, very good forgeries using warm white Ingrès drawing paper and historic inks. The same with the corks. Some were genuine Pétrus '82. Others were historic corks, hand-printed. The wine, of course, was complete crap."

"Jesus, Shawcross!" Starr exclaimed. "I saw Refeuille loading empty bottles from that tasting party at Chateau Benedictus into his trunk. I couldn't understand it at the time, but that is absolutely what he was doing." Starr remembered watching Refeuille as he sat on le Bachelet's stone bench having a quick smoke.

"It's not just here. There's increasing evidence that bottles from all the pre-auction tastings and big wine events in Hong Kong, Beijing and Shanghai, now are being smuggled out to counterfeit operations back here and all over the world. They sell the corks and capsules too. I've heard Christie's are now publicly smashing the bottles after their pre-auction tastings, it's become such a widespread problem."

"So are the police onto Refeuille?"

"Aye. They've been watching him for months. They know he's involved but there is clearly a whole operation, a mafia if you like. That's why the DCF and the detectives are a bit pissed off that your flic Dacour arrested him for having a mobile phone in poor taste."

"We are talking murder, Jim."

"I know, I'm sorry. But the police have to get further up the food chain to stop this and Refeuille, he's no mastermind."

"It ties up with Sylvie's Romanée-Conti '45 experience too."

"Well yes, Burgundy has suffered even more than claret. But this is big, Franklin. Millions of euros; an international chain of operation. And it goes well beyond the whole scandal involving Chateau Lafite 2008."

"The lucky 8, yes, I remember reading about that. Huge Chinese interest in the vintage because of the special significance of the number 8 and then floods of counterfeits to meet demand."

"A *scandale*, as the French say. Potentially this puts the fine wine trade, which is, let's face it, 90 per cent Bordeaux appelations, on the line. A trade worth $4 billion. Not to mention my bloody job."

Starr laughed and soon had Shawcross laughing too.

It was then Starr heard his cellphone vibrate in his trouser pocket. It was Dacour.

"Oui, 'allo Erik. Comment ça va?"

"Badly," said the detective. "Refeuille has escaped."

"What? How did that happen?"

"He asked to visit the *grandes murailles*, the ruined arches where the victim's body..."

"Yes, yes," Starr interjected, impatient.

"I was there with two of my team and Christiane Montreux too, but he gave us the slip. He tricked us and disappeared."

"How can you lose a suspect like that? Wasn't he cuffed?"

"No. He has not been charged, so no. The worst of it is that we hadn't even interrogated him yet, and as we suspected, some text messages have been deleted from Madamoiselle Janneau's phone."

"Why are you telling me this?"

"I want that you keep a look out for him. He cannot be far. He may be hiding in one of the tunnels under Saint-Emilion. We have sniffer dogs searching, but somehow I think we will fail to find him. Please call me immediately if you see him. That is important. We have reason to think he may now be armed. *Compris?*"

Dacour hung up.

Shawcross raised an eyebrow and Starr said, "Refeuille has escaped — he gave the police the slip."

Silence fell between the two friends as they both took contemplative slugs of the strong coffee and allowed the news to sink in.

"Would you be interested to come with me to the Pessac lab? I don't think they'd mind a crossword compiler trailing along."

"Sure. When do we go?"

Shawcross took his car keys out of his coat pocket and jangled them in front of Starr.

"Ah. I just remembered. I've arranged to meet Cappucine Montélimar. She's a friend of Madame de Cazaux and provided her alibi. Do you know her?"

"Everyone knows Cappucine. I'm surprised you've not met her, Franklin. Maybe I can phone the Pessac lab and come with. You don't think she's mixed up in this murder do you?"

"I don't know. There's something in the 'private life of Sylvie' file that is a mystery, and maybe she can help us explain it."

Five minutes' later, Starr was screwing up his face and hitting the virtual brake with his right foot as Shawcross drove the powerful 7-series

BMW at breakneck speeds along the narrow D2 towards Saint-Emilion and Chateau Beauséjour.

The brilliant blue skies of the morning were now accentuated by scudding white clouds, like the background to the credits for *The Simpsons*, thought Starr, and a wind was whipping through the tender new vine tendrils. As the narrow lane twisted and turned you could catch glimpses, through the poplar copses and farmhouses, of the great sleepy Dordogne, curving through the broad river bed below them to the Garonne and eventually the sea. She was like a satiated lover, thought Starr, stretching out naked on her flat, green bed.

A sudden downpour came out of nowhere and Shawcross turned on his wipers with a little too much gusto so that they flicked backwards and forwards over the windscreen in frenetic, fast-forward motion. It was still deluging as they turned through the stone pillars of the entrance to Chateau Beauséjour, up the short drive to the mellow square house beyond. The shutters were painted in traditional ox blood red and a couple of chocolate labradors ambled from their perch under the dry porch at the top of the house's stone steps, to greet them.

Starr unfolded a supermarket plastic bag from his coat pocket where he always kept it and putting it on his head, got out of the car to pat the labs a bit gingerly because he didn't feel entirely comfortable with dogs. Steam was rising from the sun-toasted ground and even in the rain it was warm. Just then the perfect arc of a rainbow appeared over the house. If you'd been superstitious you'd have taken it as an omen.

A figure came hurrying towards them from the vineyard to the left of the house.

"What weather!" said Starr.

"You know what they say. There's no bad weather, just bad clothes!" answered the figure whom they could now see, was a woman in her mid-forties dressed like a farm labourer, hair tied back with a piece of garden twine, feet sensibly shod in workmen's boots.

Having been had before at the de Cazaux's flat, Starr speculated on whether or not she was indeed the legendary Cappucine Montélimar. He didn't have to wait long for Shawcross, squeezing himself out of the huge car like toothpaste, hollered,

"Cappucine – I hope you don't mind. I couldn't resist coming along with my old friend, Franklin Starr. He is an American but has lived up at Sainte Croix for a while so is at least semi-tamed!"

Starr looked more closely at the woman in front of him. She had an open, tanned face, with soft brown eyes and fine bone structure. She stood tall and rangy, maybe 5 foot 10, and had a firm, but not crushing handshake.

"Please, won't you come in," she welcomed them not up the front stone steps but down the side of the house to a rear entrance into a boot room, where gumboots, a selection of coats, hats and gloves were informally spread about. Here Cappucine kicked off her boots and hung her coat up, loosened her rather beautiful wild hair and set about washing her hands in a traditional stone sink, carved from a solid piece of stone.

"It's quite dreadful, this business of Sylvie Janneau," she said. She spoke English very fluently, with an accent of course, but a mild one. As if reading his thoughts she continued, "I hope you don't mind my speaking English. I get so little opportunity to practise it, but I know you probably want to practise your French too!"

"No, it's great. You speak really excellent English. Where did you learn it?"

"Don't laugh, Monsieur Starr, but actually in Australia. I spent four years learning how to make wine and the English came along as a side benefit."

"Well you don't sound Australian, does she, Jim?"

"You're all foreigners to my ear," said the Lancastrian. "There are so few of us left who speak the Queen's English. Really a dying breed." He bent his hoary head in a melodramatic pose.

"I'm ready for a glass of wine. Will you join me?" Cappucine asked.

"Only if it's one of yours," said Shawcross.

"I drink nothing else."

They had by now walked through some stone passages to a large and bright kitchen. A white enamel jug with a bunch of flowers, picked from the garden, Starr had no doubt, stood on the scrubbed table.

"I knew Sylvie of course," said Cappucine, opening a bottle of the 2002 Beauséjour with aplomb. "She and Marie-Joëlle came here at least twice to stay for the weekend, you know."

"What was your impression of her?" asked Starr.

"Well, compared to us, of course she was so young. A different generation. But she had a quite outstanding gift with wine, an instinct. Of that there was no doubt. I can honestly say I have never met someone, especially someone in their 20s whose palate was so responsive, so nuanced."

"Was she the first of Marie-Joëlle's, ahm, extra-marital affairs?" asked Starr.

Cappucine set down the tray she had been assembling.

"No, not the first, Monsieur Starr. Marie-Joëlle is the kind of woman who always has a lover. It is like breathing for her. I've known her since we were 11, and it has never changed. We were at the Sacré Coeur in Blaye together."

"So you are both Catholic?"

"*Bien sur.* Of course."

The two men followed Cappucine into the great old house's dining room. It was less grand than the salon, with a large round table in the middle and French windows looking out across the Chateau's vineyards. A handsome French oak buffet occupied the length of one wall and the original stone fireplace another. "This room gets the midday sun so I thought we might be more comfortable here," Cappucine said.

"I have so many questions. I hardly know where to start," Starr said.

"I am at your service," she smiled.

"Let's start with you. How did you come to buy Beauséjour?"

"My story is really quite simple. I grew up just south of Bergerac. My parents made vinegar, not wine. They still do. I am of peasant stock, you see. In the 1970s, their little artisan business grew with the increased interest in Mediterranean cooking in northern Europe and they started to develop the range into flavoured vinegars. For the first time they had money. My brother was always destined to be a vinegar-maker, but my father had different ambitions for me. They sent me away to be educated by the nuns, and that's where I met Marie-Joëlle. Of course our backgrounds were poles apart, but, there was err a closeness between us that has remained."

There was a long silence then she continued.

"After school, I went to Bordeaux University and my first degree was in History of Art, but I was always fascinated by wine, especially the wines of the Médoc and Saint-Emilion. So I went to wine school and then to Australia. At that time, the best wine-makers were not to be found among the chateaux of the grand cru classés here, but in Southern Australia. I was building my knowledge before having the confidence to buy here and start my own little project."

"How on earth did you finance it? I know Beauséjour was run-down, and is a small estate, but the investment must have been considerable. I hope you don't mind my asking?" Starr was increasingly intrigued.

"Some of the money came from my parents. They had built up some savings, you know, and since my brother will inherit the vinegar business, I had my share of the inheritance early."

"And the rest?"

"The rest came from Marie-Joëlle. As you will know, Monsieur Starr, she comes from a very large fragrance family – one of the largest in France – and money was never a problem for her."

"So does she retain an interest, a stake, in Beauséjour?"

"Oh not formally, no. It was all a gift. But she remains interested in how the estate performs. She was here for the *en primeur* when Sylvie was, err, murdered."

Starr was struck by how Cappucine Montélimar was like a perfect mirror image of Marie-Joëlle. Cappucine was open and direct, while Marie-Joëlle was closed and defensive. And yet, thought Starr, it's the dark side of the moon that draws me. Cappucine was like a guy – a guy you'd go for a few beers with, uncomplicated, straight up.

"So when did Marie-Joëlle decide to come and stay?"

"This last time? She called from the train; perhaps a few hours before I met her at Libourne station."

"Was that typical of her? I mean to just turn up like that. And why didn't she stay at the Plaisance with her husband?" Starr asked and took a swallow of the fabulous, rounded red wine. The wine was big and generous, aromatic, with some truffles among the intense earthy flavours. After the full black cherries of the fruit, Starr marvelled at the long, smooth finish. This was a wine of perfect balance and great subtlety: a wine of the very first order that would be drinking well for another decade.

"Bloody hell, Franklin. Let the poor woman draw breath. It's like machinegun fire with all these questions. Cappucine, I apologise for my American friend's lack of manners," Shawcross frowned at Starr.

"Oh that's alright, Jim. We are all anxious to know who killed Sylvie. I quite understand. I think Gilles was quite tied up with meetings for *Cuvée*. It's a busy time for him. It isn't unusual for Marie-Joëlle and he to arrange their lives separately."

"Can you just tell me what happened on that Thursday – the day of Sylvie's murder?"

"I met the TGV at about 12.30 and we came back here for lunch. Marie-Joëlle had texted Sylvie to let her know she was here and to make an arrangement to meet up. Sylvie was already committed for that evening. She was having dinner with a négociant – one Monsieur Shawcross will know – Damien Refeuille. Sylvie borrowed my car and went into Saint-Emilion in the afternoon. I don't know if she and Sylvie met up, but I know she hoped to see her at the funny little hotel she was staying at."

"Le Petit Girondine?" asked Starr.

"Yes. Do you know it?"

"A long time ago, yes."

"So when did she get back here?"

"As I told the police, she was here for dinner at about 8.30pm and we chatted and then went to bed."

"At what time?" asked Starr.

"Oh perhaps 11pm or 11.15pm."

"And you next saw her in the morning for breakfast?"

"Yes of course. Monsieur Starr, you cannot seriously think Marie-Joëlle would have wished Sylvie any harm?"

"Of course not. I'm sorry to sound so accusatory, I really am."

Starr fell quiet and looked pensively out of the beautiful triple aspect French windows to the landscape beyond.

"I am beginning to get used to it. The police have been here asking questions very similar to yours. But they seemed very anxious to know if Marie-Joëlle suffered from insomnia; if she took sleeping tablets."

Starr concentrated. "Really? And did she?"

"No, as I told the *inspecteur*, Marie-Joëlle is the kind of woman who is very careful what she eats. I doubt that she even takes an aspirin for a headache!"

A quiet descended on the dining room, Cappucine, Jim and Starr each cocooned in a private thought.

"It's beautiful here," said Starr breaking the silence and gazing across the manicured vineyard, each row of vines marked at its end with a single red rose bush.

"And the rain has stopped. Shall we have a quick look at the chai?"

With that, the two men followed Saint-Emilion's most famed female winemaker out to the large stone barn, the two chocolate labradors bringing up the rear like a formal procession. The chai's vaulted ceiling and vast cold space gave the impression of a great Romanesque cathedral, which, thought Starr, it kind of was.

They were only about half way down the first row of oak barrels when Starr's cellphone vibrated. Apologising to the others, he strode to take the call outside.

"We've lost him again," said Dacour.

"Lost who?"

"Refeuille, of course."

"Yeh I know. You told me – he gave you the slip at the Grandes Murailles," Starr began to think Dacour's mind was going.

"No, no afterwards. We traced him to the quais on the rive gauche in Bordeaux. He visited Serge Piezenski's studio and never came out. His car is still parked in the street, but he has completely disappeared."

"Who is Serge Whateverski?"

"Oh really even you must know him. He is the renowned art restorer – everyone knows him. His atelier is in the rue Ferrière not far from the quai."

"Obviously you questioned this Serge – sorry I still can't quite get his name?"

"Piezenski. Yes of course. My number two, Michel, he waited 15 minutes and then they went in. No-one was there except for a young assistant from Georgia. He spoke little French but claimed no-one had entered the atelier and that Piezenski was in Italy on business."

"And no sign of Refeuille?"

"Of course not! I knew this would happen. *Putain!* " The detective swore and hung up.

Now it was Starr's turn to use some creative thinking. He called Anaïs at the gallery.

"A Russian art restorer in the Quai Ferrière?" Starr heard Anaïs laugh out loud clearly sharing the joke with someone in the gallery.

"What's the joke?"

"Serge Piezenski is world-famous," she said. "He is probably one of the top handful of restorers in the world. There is no gallery or collector who doesn't know him and a great many masterpieces owe their life to his studio."

"Old Masters, huh?"

"Yeh, a bit like you, Franklin, but restored to their former glory, not cracked and covered in smoke."

Now it was Starr's turn to laugh.

"You think he's straight? No rumour of anything, you know, crooked?"

"Oh, you mean that affair about the forgeries?"

Starr didn't know what Anaïs was talking about but encouraged her.

"Yeah. Remind me what happened with that."

"It was all dismissed months ago, but a reporter for *Le Monde* ran a story that somewhere in Piezenski's atelier there was a master forger, doing mainly second-tier Impressionists, working from old auction catalogues where the paintings had disappeared. It was a clever idea. The accusation was works that had gone missing were being expertly forged (with aged paint, hand-made varnish, old canvas, the works) and then carefully "discovered". When the authentication process was carried out before an auction house would accept the painting was an original, of course the catalogue entry, matching the painting precisely offered positive confirmation. But it was never proved you know. Are we still meeting for lunch?"

"Yes absolutely – the terrace at CAPC – 13.30."

As Starr turned into the chai, he saw Shawcross in deep discussion with the renowned wine-maker, the two united by a common passion, a common obsession.

"Give me a lift to Bordeaux, Jim? I'll have to come to the Pessac lab another time. Something's come up."

"Something five feet ten tall with fine bone structure and a long lunch hour, by any chance?"

"Ha. Ha. Yes I am meeting Anaïs for lunch. Real lunch not 'lunch,'" Starr finger mimed quotation marks in the air.

Shawcross raised his spectacular eyebrows at Capuccine in disbelief and all three walked to the car.

CHAPTER

8

S tarr liked the terrace restaurant of the CAPC in Bordeaux. It was so typical of the French to get none other than Andrée Putman to design the interior with its huge golden lighting adding drama to the vaulted stone arches. Down below, among the grand limestone columns, its early history as the old customs house was preserved in confident, imperialist splendour. Here the exotic imports from the colonies – cocoa, sugar, coffee, spices – would be stored before being traded throughout northern Europe. Not all contemporary art museums had the panache of the CAPC, and few could match its terrace restaurant, for views, food, wine or clientèle, even if Anaïs was dismissive of the collection.

There was the usual clutch of what Anaïs called the AAs – a tribe they both despised, although, Starr thought, probably for different reasons – but also a convivial gaggle of students, latter-day revolutionaries, and even the odd chateau owner. Today the place was full and Anaïs was almost at the table before Starr spotted her, head held high, statement jewellery gleaming like stolen treasure against the velvet of her skin. Her beauty shocked Starr. He found it hard to digest, somehow. He poured half his glass of wine – a restrained but pleasant Graves – into her glass and chinked: a practice she found vulgar but amusing.

She swivelled her head round on her long neck, clocking one or two art advisers, the detested AAs, smiling and nodding to half a dozen people she knew. Starr was continually impressed by her memory for faces and names. While 99 per cent of people he met he forgot, for Anaïs, the ratio was reversed. Having performed a full sweep of the busy terrace, she turned her attention to Starr.

"So Franklin, what's all this about Piezenski? I feel you need to catch me up."

"Let's order first," said Starr, suddenly hungry.

He chose a *velouté* of courgettes with fresh mint and parmesan crisps to start while Anaïs went for the charcuterie, as usual, and then they both chose a sirloin steak with pesto and salad for the main.

"Shall we share some frites?" Anaïs asked.

"Good idea," said Starr, his stomach rumbling.

"So is Serge Piezenski your chief suspect, Mister Holmes?"

Starr told Anaïs everything he himself knew, as they munched through their first courses, the bottle of Graves steadily emptying.

"What do you think, Anaïs?"

"I don't think a woman would do that. It has to be a man. And I think it has to be a man who wanted to send a message. It's a very dramatic place, *les grandes murailles*. I think whoever did this did it to send a warning; a warning that everyone would understand. I don't think it's a personal thing."

"Hang on, what did you say? About a message?"

"Well if you just want to kill someone to get them out of the way, you, I don't know, shoot them with a silencer and dump the body in the river, or you arrange some kind of fatal accident. Whoever murdered Sylvie wanted her to be discovered. It was a public killing. Almost like an execution," Anaïs sipped her wine and fiddled with her large rings, turning them round her long, elegant fingers.

"You know you are absolutely right," said Starr. "It's nothing personal. I kept thinking how odd it was to see her poor body hanging on the old ruins, but you're right. That choice was deliberate."

"Yeh, but who needed to make that statement and why?"

"Mmm. You tell me the why and I'll tell you the who, as they say."

Starr was just thinking about a chocolate mousse he saw flash past him to another table when the light on his phone flashed to indicate he had a new text message.

It was from a number he didn't recognise. "La Maison Sainte Marie, Cadillac. Urgent." Starr called the number but there was no reply and no voicemail.

"I'm going to have to go. Can I borrow your car?" he pleaded with Anaïs.

"So much for our leisurely lunch. Yes that's fine. I don't need the car, but please be careful with her. Just call me later, OK?" She put the keys into the palm of his hand and taking his other hand, cradled his hands in hers just for a moment. Desire flickered through his body, but it was no good. He had to find out what had happened in Cadillac.

Starr kissed her on the mouth and left a wad of 20-euro notes on the table to cover the bill.

He was over the bridge and out onto the motorway within ten minutes then branching off south following the Garonne through the narrow lanes, just-green vineyards, little coppices and clustered old hamlets until he came to the ancient bastide town nestling on her banks.

As he drove, he pondered on the ironic misconnection with Detroit. The one-time powerhouse of automobile history had, of course, been founded by Antoine de Lamothe-Cadillac and you'd be forgiven for assuming he hailed from Cadillac. But Lamothe-Cadillac was no Girondin but a native of the Tarn, adopting the name in a random quirk. He had no more legitimate connection with the ancient Girondine port than Starr himself. The all-American luxury limo and this small old village on the banks of the Garonne would be forever connected by a name, a word that implied kinship that never was. *L'habit ne fait pas le moine*, he thought. All is not what it seems.

As the large stone ramparts of the old town came into view, the chateau de Cadillac towered above the small town dominating the vineyards that stretched in every direction beneath its scalloped roof slates. Power, thought Starr, power that inspires and threatens in equal measure, oozed from its towers and parterres. Jean-Louis Nogaret de la Valette, the first duke d'Epernon, certainly understood power and hired architects capable of expressing its magnetism in this mass of honeyed stone: a fortified palace for a little king.

The Maison Sainte Marie nursing home was well-signposted and lay up a pleasant gravelled drive on the outskirts of the bastide town. Landscaped lawns, planted with large marine pines and chestnut trees, surrounded the mellow stone house at their centre. Several elderly people, patients presumably, were walking with zimmer frames along the well-maintained gravel walkways. Starr parked in the area designated for 'visiteurs' and without locking the car, ran up the shallow stone steps to the reception desk.

"And you are here to see?" asked the impassive face of the receptionist, her face doubly removed by the glass panel of the reception booth and her red-framed spectacles.

Starr's heart sank. He had no idea what he was here to see. He'd have to wing it.

"I am an expert advisor to the police," he improvised. She looked at him long and hard and without responding lifted the receiver of her switchboard phone and dialled.

"*Carte d'identité?*" she said.

Starr pulled his passport, that he was never without, from the inside pocket of his jacket.

"Monsieur Franklin Starr, *Américain*," the receptionist added the epithet as an expletive, after her laborious pronunciation of his name and replaced the telephone into its base station.

"Along the corridor to the right. Take the third door on the left. Someone will meet you there. *Passez une bonne soirée*," she said, on autopilot. Have a nice day, French style.

Starr was acutely aware of his footsteps echoing on the polished linoleum floors that smelled of institutions and disinfectant as he swung through the fire doors to he wasn't sure what.

The plastic yellow police tape and the sudden rush of uniformed police told him that whatever was the reason for the visit to the nursing home, they had all arrived too late.

He waited patiently taking in police photographers, a forensics team and comings and goings focused on a room beyond, whose door was open but whose contents were obscured from his view.

Christiane was there and waved to him. She ducked under the tape and taking him by his arm nodded to the policeman guarding the corridor.

"We arrived too late," she said without emotion.

"Who is it?" asked Starr.

"The mother of Damien Refeuille. You didn't know?"

Starr frowned. "I got a text message. Did you send it?"

The police officer shook her head.

"Did *you* know that Refeuille's mother was here?" asked Starr.

"Yes, I, err we have known for a while. But it was only when he escaped that we thought to come here. We arrived perhaps ten minutes too late, not more. Cardiac massage failed to revive her."

The bright little room gave little away. At its centre was a hospital bed with a cornflower blue blanket. Dangling next to it was a cord attached to a red patient alarm. The sheet had been pulled over the incumbent's head and a stretcher was about to take the body away. Clearly both forensics and police photography had finished with her. There was a small flatscreen TV on an angled bracket on the wall and on the top of the bedside table a single framed photograph of a couple in their thirties and standing between them a boy and a girl, either twins or very close in age.

"Was she?" Starr didn't end the question.

"No. It looks like a heart attack. We'll know for sure after the post-mortem, but nothing to suggest violence," said Christiane.

Starr saw then that there was a French window that led from the room onto a wrap-around terrace with ironically cheerful pots of geraniums. It was open. If it had been his room, he'd have kept the French window open to counteract the oppressive heat of the nursing home.

Dacour, looking particularly drawn and grey, burst into the room and barked at Starr, "What are you doing here? Who let you cross the police barrier?"

Before he had time to think of a response, Christiane intervened.

"He is with me, *Capitaine*. It is my fault. He has not touched anything," she said.

"Well make sure he doesn't," was the detective's response. "It looks like natural causes but until the autopsy we treat it as a potential crime scene. *Compris?*"

Christiane spoke to Starr. "We've taken the CCTV tapes from the car-park camera, but I'm not holding my breath. This time it does look like a natural death, after all."

"How old was she?" Starr asked the two policemen, calculating that if Refeuille was say 40ish, his mother could only have been perhaps 65; no age to be in a nursing home.

"Not old – 68," replied Dacour. "But she had a bad heart and suffered from chronic insomnia. She was not a healthy woman."

"Insomnia?"

"Yes, insomnia. When you cannot sleep, Starr."

"I know what the word means, Dacour. Is that significant?"

"Why do you ask?" Dacour stood at the open French window with his back to Christiane and Starr.

"Cappucine Montélimar mentioned that you had asked if Madame de Cazaux suffered from insomnia. I thought there must be a link."

Dacour turned round to face Starr across the now empty white wrought iron bed. Without saying a word he left the room and headed purposefully down the pine-scented corridor.

"Let's go," said Christiane to Starr. "If I stay, Dacour will have me question all the staff and all the old folks in the rooms on either side of Madame Refeuille. I really hate all that routine plodwork," she smiled. "Can I buy you a drink in Cadillac?"

For all the world Starr thought she was flirting with him, or perhaps pretending to flirt with him more likely, but why? Was it she who had called him here? Who else knew his mobile number? But why? Something was going on but he couldn't put his finger on it.

"Another time perhaps. There's someone I want to see," he lied vaguely. Christiane smiled and, turning on a well-polished heel, clicked down the linoleum-tiled corridor, ducking under the police tape without disturbing a single black hair around her serene, perfectly made-up face.

As soon as he was sure she'd gone, Starr strolled in the opposite direction, away from the reception desk and the steps out to the car park.

The sounds of a poorly-tuned piano drifted through the over-heated, under-oxygenated air. Starr thought he recognised the final bars of Chopin's Etude in F minor; the player perfectly in control of the fast, loud arpeggios that bring the piece known as *Sunshine* to a triumphant close. He followed the sound to a large general sitting room, open on two sides to the gardens and filled with empty chairs arranged in an expectant semi-circle. The tinkler of the ivories had his back to Starr but he was unmistakable, even in this most unlikely of settings.

"Why Monsieur de Bachelet," Starr tried not to splutter, "What on earth are you doing here?"

Before the elegant aristocrat had a chance to reply, a plump, middle-aged woman in the nursing home's café-au-lait uniform burst through the double swing doors.

"Monsieur de Bachelet! No-one told me you had arrived already. I would have brought you some coffee, some biscuits, or a tisane?" she added nervously.

The chateau owner stood up from the piano stool and reassured the care-worker with effortless charm, a charm honed over several centuries during which countless women just like the nursing home worker had melted, as softened metal, to the firey will of the de Bachelets.

"I'm sorry. I just slipped in through the garden windows, for a secret bit of practice. My playing is so *rouillé*, so very rusty, and I am so anxious not to disappoint the audience, he bowed slightly. Only then did Starr see that the room was not entirely empty. In the final row of chairs at the back of the large, light room, he winced as the loud English woman from de Bachelet's wine tasting party oiled her way towards him.

"Oh Ghee," she gushed, carefully pronouncing his name in the French manner. "That was magnificent. A treat. We were lost in the experience, weren't we Norman?" She turned to gather validation from her silent shadow of a husband. "You should play professionally, shouldn't he Norman?" Norman remained impassive. He looked as though he might himself have expired many decades before and been preserved, like Lenin, in the formaldehyde of his sterile marriage.

Before the swirling thoughts that clouded Starr's brain had had a chance of settling, the double doors were opened to a voluble group of clashing zimmer frames, wheelchairs and walking sticks: a gaggle of scoliotic spines. Excitement and anticipation filled the room and from the general cheerfulness Starr assumed none of Madame Refeuille's fellow residents had yet learned that, just as they squabbled over their seating positions, her lifeless body was being delivered to the Libourne morgue.

Try as he might, there was no escaping the appalling English woman. She enveloped him in a mist of floral fragrance, her small podgy hands on his arm, the Schiaperelli-pink nails, like shiny burrowing beetles, digging into his shirtsleeve. She was in full flow, declaiming loudly about de Bachelet's selfless support of the Maison Sainte Marie, how last year he'd gotten some Bordeaux art expert to conduct a little art auction, the year before there had been a visit to his chais, how every year there was an event to raise money for the nursing home, all personally organised by de Bachelet himself. Wasn't that amazing? Starr was adept at appearing engaged while 95 per cent of his mind wandered off elsewhere. The accent irritated him. The woman irritated him. The fawning adulation irritated him. He smiled sweetly.

Salvation arrived at last in the form of the Maison Sainte Marie manager who gestured them into a chair and silence. Mumbling his excuses, Starr dived for the doors and loped up the corridor, as the muffled sounds of Chopin's arching arpeggios conveyed its message of optimism to the infirm and dying. The place appeared deserted: everyone was apparently sequestered in the makeshift concert hall.

But not quite all as it turned out. A cleaner was wielding a heavy floor polisher down the corridors as Starr rounded a corner, almost colliding with her.

"*Excusez-moi*," he said.

"No problem, nothing broken." The cleaner spoke French with a strong African accent – Congo, Mozambique? – Starr wasn't sure. She was large, her hair braided like fine marquetry on her head, and intelligence flickered in her deep brown eyes.

"Are you just starting work or is this the end of your shift?" Starr tried to sound casually conversational.

"You a cop?" she asked.

"Hell no," said Starr. "I'm just...just a friend. Of Madame Refeuille's."

"You aint no friend, Sir. I never seen you here before. You never visited. What's your interest?"

"OK. My interest is in Madame Refeuille's son, Damien. Did you know him?"

"Sure. I know him. He's here every week. Regular as the watch on your arm, Sir. A good mama's boy," she let out a huge, explosive laugh. "Here for his mama."

"Did you happen to notice, I mean in general, whether Madame Refeuille was in the habit of opening her French windows; perhaps for fresh air?" asked Starr.

"Madame Refeuille wasn't ill," the cleaner replied. "She could walk about. But she slept a lot in the daytime. Sure, sometimes her doors would be open."

"Thank you, err, sorry, I don't know your name."

"You can call me Oriane. Everyone calls me Oriane."

"*Au revoir* Oriane, and thank you for your help. Really very helpful."

The heavy disinfectant-laden air was making Starr feel nauseous. Time to go, he thought, and tried to find his way back to the reception desk and the exit. After a number of wrong turns, he found the entrance hall with relief and was soon breathing in the fresh air sweetened with the smell of cut grass, a cigarette in his hand. He paced the gravelled paths that surrounded the maison de retraite, something unconscious keeping him there, but what he didn't know.

The gardens were typical of French institutions: mainly laid to rough grass with cedars and marine pines providing interest and shade. A few lilac trees and hibiscus were in leaf but not yet flower. Somewhere in the distance a clock chimed. Bees hummed. It was the picture of tranquillity and calm, not a bad place to end your days.

Suddenly Starr knew what had kept him from leaving. He stubbed out his half-finished cigarette on the gravel and bounded up the stone steps back to the unbending receptionist. She gave him a cool stare through the double-glazing of her glass kiosk and her red-rimmed spectacles, but he decided to ignore her and walked briskly past through a set of fire doors into the torrid heat of the corridors.

He soon caught up with Oriane, swaying as she pushed the floor polisher from wall to wall in rhythmic, hypnotic circles.

"When did you last see him?" asked Starr.

"Who, Monsieur Refeuille?"

Starr nodded, impatient now.

"He was here today, this morning."

"Why didn't you say?" Starr was angry as much with himself as the woman who had now stopped her polisher and was resting one generous arm on it.

"Why didn't you ask?"

Starr looked at the cleaning woman again and wondered what other questions he had failed to ask.

"Do you happen to know if Madame Refeuille kept any of her medications in her room?" he chanced.

"You mean her pills? Sure, she kept them back for her boy."

"Oriane: are you saying Madame Refeuille's son was stealing pills from her? What pills?"

"Them white pills is what he wanted. He's not the only one either. Reckon half the old folks' medications slip out through these doors," she thumbed towards the entrance hall behind her.

"One man's morphine is another man's heroine, Monsieur Starr. Hospitals, nursing homes – they are just candy stores. Where there's candy, there's cash. Monsieur Refeuille's mama thought the world of her boy. She'd have stolen the *Tour Eiffel* if he'd asked her."

"How do you know this? Did Madame Refeuille discuss it with you?"

"Don't be silly. Monsieur. I'm just a cleaner. No-one sees me; no-one talks to me except to tell me how to do my job. But I got eyes, Monsieur. You don't have to be told something to know it. I see things, plenty of things. She put her pills in her spare spectacle case, not her regular case, but the one she kept her spare reading specs in. It's blue. In the drawer of her bedside table. See for yourself."

Starr retraced his steps back through the featureless corridors to the police tape. The uniformed cops were still there and there was no way he was going to be able to get past them or check out the cleaner's story. He dialled Dacour on his cell.

"Starr?"

Starr had no more than five minutes to wait before his cell vibrated and Dacour confirmed that there was a blue glasses case in the drawer of Madame Refeuille's bedside table, and it had a pair of glasses and nothing else in it. Forensics had bagged the case and would check for fingerprints and trace, but, Dacour kept saying, "natural causes, Starr, natural causes."

Before he left, there were two questions he had to put to Oriane.

"Oriane, I saw that Madame Refeuille had a photograph in her room of two children, a girl and a boy. Am I right in thinking she had a daughter as well as a son?"

Oriane stopped her polisher and stood for a moment staring carefully at Starr.

"That's very smart of you, Sir. Yes she had twins, but no-one knows where the daughter is. She's never visited, never written. I think they must be estranged. Or maybe she lives in Australia or somewheres."

"Thanks. And finally, do you remember what time this morning you saw Damien Refeuille? Did you see him leave?" he asked.

Oriane stopped the noisy machine once more.

"You aint helping me get my work done, Sir," she said. "But I can see what you're thinking and you're wrong. Yes I saw Monsieur Refeuille leave. He ran round the back of the building, avoiding the main entrance. But I know he would never have hurt his mama," she said.

"Well that's what everyone thinks until a murder is proved," said Starr dubiously.

"Not in this case, Sir. She was as alive as you are now when he left. Of that I can assure you. I cleaned her room, see," and with that she turned away from Starr and resumed the sonorous whirring of the polisher.

CHAPTER

9

As Starr's beat-up old Peugeot coughed its way into the small driveway of La Borie, Jim Shawcross was expertly nudging the cork from a bottle of Billecart-Salmon rosé. He poured the exquisite bubbling champagne into two flutes.

"What's the occasion?" asked Starr as he joined the dishevelled old wine buyer on the terrace.

Ignoring the question, Shawcross drank a good half glass, breathed deeply and quoted Dorothy Parker in theatrical tones: "Three be the things I shall never attain: envy, content and sufficient Champagne."

"That's the first time I've heard you quote poetry – well rhyme," Starr frowned. "Is everything alright?"

"It's been better," Shawcross swayed his head from side to side. "But I'm off and thought we'd have a valedictory *coupe*."

"Off where – back to the drizzle of London?"

"Eventually, but via Hong Kong." Shawcross stared meaningfully at Starr, who, if he expected further explanation, was to be disappointed.

Starr tilted his glass in a silent half-toast to his friend and swallowed the salmony-pink, lightly bubbling wine. The two men had long agreed that they'd trade all the bling of the biggest, brashest Champagne brands for this traditional family-owned house. The Billecarts had been making champagne from their small vineyard holding for over 200 years – long enough for Napoleon to have drunk it in exile on St Helena, had the British been kind enough to send him some.

"Lovely," said Starr. "So are you going to tell me what you're going for? Or is this another one of your secrets?"

"No secret, no. The office has roped me into doing some glitzy tasting classes at the Mandarin Oriental, you know. They've got 12 Bordeaux chateaux, each presenting their seven best vintages, and me, poor sods. It happens to coincide with this, though..." He fumbled in his jacket pocket and handed Starr a scrappy folded pink page torn from the *Financial Times*.

"'Important Bordeaux from a Private Cellar,'" read Starr. "'Mouton-Rothschild 1982, Cheval Blanc 1982, Lynch-Bages 1979,'" the list continued. At the bottom of the notice it simply had the famous auctioneer's address at One Pacific Place, Hong Kong.

"Are you buying or investigating?"

"Neither. I leave the amateur sleuthing to you, and Williams & Williams never buys pre-2000 wines that aren't cellared by us. You should know that. The Mouton will go for a hysterical price," he said. "There's just not enough ready-to-drink fine vintage claret available to meet Chinese demand. The sky's the limit."

The two men shared an unspoken thought in comfortable silence.

"Anyway I'd better shift my bottom if I'm to make the plane and grab myself a cardboard butty from the airport," Shawcross swallowed down the remains of his glass, and giving Starr his trademark bear slap on the back, heaved his large frame across the terrace down to his gleaming black car.

"She suits you," he said.

"Who? What?"

"The Guadeloupe goddess, Starr – Anaïs isn't it?"

Starr had not broadcast his new relationship, mainly because he didn't want to jinx it, and couldn't quite believe it was real, himself. Shawcross was a wily old SOB, though.

"Luckiest man alive," he said.

The engine purring, Shawcross had slammed the gearstick violently into reverse when he pushed the button to slide down the driver's window and barked, "I almost forgot. The office sent me a new iPhone, so once I work out how to turn the bloody thing on, I'll text you, Starr. Keep you abreast, so to speak..." His voice, as hoarse and bristly as the Lancastrian moors, was soon engulfed by the revving straight six of his hired BMW, as it lurched backwards through the gateposts and sped up the narrow lane in a cloud of chalky dust.

Starr lit a Camel Light and returned to the bottle of Billecart with the trace of a plan to make a start on a movie-themed crossword he had agreed to do – more as a favour to his first ever boss than for its remuneration, which was paltry. 'Sorry, go on mate!' he thought and scribbled down the clue in his wine-tasting book.

He was just about to fill his glass when he noticed a folded-up newspaper cutting on the ground. It must have dropped from Shawcross's pocket when he pulled out the Sotheby's wine auction notice. It was in Mandarin, but there was a photo showing several cases of Lafitte, four Chinese officials in identikit suits, a tall, patrician figure (presumably the auctioneer), a slim woman with a blonde bob and Shawcross. Starr took the magnifying glass he always carried, since his reading glasses had an irritating tendency to wander off, and examined the photo. It was poor quality newsprint but there was something very familiar about the woman, and yet wrong too. His mind snapped shut over the answer like a sprung trap.

At that moment his cellphone buzzed and he ran up to the far edge of his garden, where it gave way as if in defeat to the marching armies of vines, to answer it.

"Starr."

"Monsieur Starr. It is Marie-Joëlle de Cazaux. You remember you came to our *leedle* apartment in Paris?" The upward inflection and timbre of her voice needed no further introduction.

"Of course I remember. How can I be of assistance?" What was it about the European upper crust that automatically made you doff your verbal cap and tug at your verbal forelock, he thought. His instinctive deference sickened the democrat in him.

"I am here in Saint-Emilion with my old friend Cappucine and wonder if I could come and see you. I have received rather a shock," she continued.

"Shock?"

"I would prefer not to discuss this on the telephone, Monsieur Starr. It is a *leedle*delicate. But perhaps you would allow me to buy you a drink in town?"

"Err...well, umm," Starr hesitated.

"I see I 'ave again robbed you of the power of speech," she said.

"No, err, I was just thinking of my schedule," he lied.

"Ah of course. The crowded social *calendrier* of the crossword creator." The tumbling rocks of her French 'r's were as fatally attractive to Starr as was the sarcasm.

"Let me know when and where and I'll be there," he managed to get out.

"Let's say *Les Trois Etoiles*, do you know eet? In 'alf an hour?"

"OK, yes I know it. *A toute à l'heure*," he was still speaking when he realised she'd hung up.

He glanced at his faded jeans, his clean but un-ironed Brooks Brothers shirt with its worn cuffs, and his three-summers-old espadrilles. He had just enough time to jump in the shower, give himself a quick shave and man up for the match.

Starr chose a table not right at the back but about half way down the narrow little bar above which Sylvie had said Refeuille had his office. The tape on the bell told him that the police had sealed it up. He'd ordered himself a glass of Perrier: he knew this woman's power to disorientate, to force a compass error, and wanted to drop anchor and prevent himself from drifting out of his depth. He hadn't long to wait.

"Ah Monsieur Starr, *bonsoir*, you shouldn't have changed for me," she greeted him. She was wearing a long fine linen top, cut low, over cropped, narrow trousers with bright blue Gucci loafers. At her throat was a triple band of natural pearls that reflected the turquoise and green of her shirt and her eyes. She managed to look sexy, stylish and yet casual – it was a difficult trick to pull off.

"And 'ow interesting. I would not have associated you with Green Irish Tweed – such a classic, English fragrance for such an American man."

"I don't think I'm *such* an American," Starr felt he'd been insulted, but wasn't sure how. "But I'm impressed. I'm hardly wearing it. Can you identify anybody's cologne?" he asked.

"Monsieur Starr, my family has been making fragrances for over two centuries. It would be strange if some of that heritage had not rubbed off on me, don't you think?" She glanced up at him flirtatiously and he felt the involuntary ripple of desire begin to unravel him.

"Pierre Bourdon has never admitted to creating the famous Creed fragrance," she continued. "But I 'appen to know he was closely involved, and Cary Grant was the first person to wear it and make it, I suppose, an instant *classique*," she paused and locked eyes with Starr. "What would you like to drink?"

"I'm in your hands," he said.

"Yes..."

Starr resented playing the role of conversational underdog and decided on attack.

"So, you are here again on your own, without your husband?" he asked rhetorically.

"Apparently yes," she said, not a bit perturbed. "Gilles is going to one of his boring Sciences-Po reunion weekends at the Chateau de Sanse. I absolutely refuse to join him." She smiled sweetly.

"Ah right," Starr fumbled. "I didn't know Gilles is a Sciences-Po graduate."

"Of course not," she said icily. "You know nothing. Nothing at all."

She had only to raise the tilt of her head to summon a waiter, instantly there for her, and then surprised Starr by ordering two glasses of Noilly Prat dry vermouth. They arrived with ice and lemon and a little plate of *amuses-bouches*.

"Chin, chin," she said raising her glass to her perfect, slim lips.

"So what's this shock you wanted to discuss?" Starr said in an effort to grab back the reins.

Marie-Joëlle lifted her almond eyes and stared deep into Starr's.

"May we be frank? I must ask for your total discretion," she said.

"Frank's my name," he said rather weakly.

"Late last night, at perhaps quarter before midnight, we heard a motorbike outside the Chai."

"At Beauséjour?"

"Yes. Cappucine and I were watching TV, so we didn't hear him coming up the approach, just when he was close."

"Him, you say? Did you see him?"

"*Patience, Monsieur.*" Marie-Joëlle raised her small hand to stop his interruptions and Starr took another swig of the lemony cold Vermouth.

"We heard the steps round to the rear entrance, where Cappucine has an outside light. Then a knock on the door. I wanted to call the police, but Cappucine is much braver than am I and put all the lights on downstairs and went to answer the door. I followed with a wine bottle in case, you know, we could..." she mimed bashing someone over the head.

"The man seemed young, but he never took off his *casque* so it was hard to see, He asked Cappucine if she was interested in buying a copy of the autopsy report for Sylvie."

"Buying?"

"500 euros. He said he could not discuss how he came by it and we had to promise not to tell the police. If we did, well, he threatened us, of course."

"So what did you do?"

"It's comic really. Cappucine started to bargain with him and eventually they agreed on 200 euros."

"So have you got it?"

Marie-Joëlle slipped a folded piece of A4 paper out of her slim poche and passed it to Starr while also almost imperceptibly ordering their drinks to be refreshed.

The photocopied report was typed on official stationery, dated and stamped. There was no doubt it was genuine. The post mortem confirmed asphyxiation consistent with hanging. No marks of resistance had been found on the body suggesting a struggle. There were no epithelials under the fingernails. Nothing to suggest homicide. The direction of the ligature mark was oblique, following the line of the jaw and the slip knot was typical – not requiring any specialist knowledge. Routine blood and urine samples had shown alcohol and a single trace of flumitrazepam or rohypnol in the femoral vein. The traces were too small to be significant and certainly not enough to cause death. No other blood samples showed any traces of the drug, just the one from the femoral vein. She had been alive when the rope tightened around her throat and effectively cut off her windpipe.

Starr read it again. Rohypnol – what the press calls the date rape drug – how could Sylvie have been drugged?

"You saw the rohypnol?" Marie-Joëlle's eyes were again full of tears that would not fall.

"That's why Dacour is so interested in insomnia."

"But it's very controlled here in France," continued Marie-Joëlle. "A friend of ours is the head pharmacist at Libourne Hospital so Cappucine called her to check. It is administered in blister packs of ten capsules and you have to have two doctors sign a prescription. Apparently the laws make it almost impossible now to find on the street."

"I can't see Sylvie experimenting with drugs, anyway," said Starr. "Can you?"

"No, absolutely not. We both were the same in that respect. But Sylvie especially was very careful not to do anything to compromise her palate. No chilli, no coffee even."

"Didn't rohypnol get slipped into drinks? It was all over the media in the 1990s. I guess if Sylvie had not been looking, Refeuille could have drugged her at his dinner with her, then walked her out to the edge of town, and, you know…"

"*Précisement*," agreed Marie-Joëlle. "But why? I don't understand how anyone would want to harm her. She was so young."

"I'm not sure, Marie-Joëlle, but I think she somehow got caught up in some wine scam. And there's another thing you should know. Refeuille's mother was found dead in her nursing-home bed earlier today and she suffered from insomnia. A cleaner said that she kept back her pills for her son. I don't know if she was prescribed rohypnol, but if she was, then that nails Refeuille. The problem is he's on the loose."

"Loose?"

"He escaped from police custody. They are so stupid, the cops. He led them to Chateau des Grandes Murailles on some fake promise and then disappeared. They picked him up again in Bordeaux but he escaped into an art restorer's studio and now he's gone."

A cloud passed across Marie-Joëlle's face at the mention of the old ruined convent.

"They'll never catch him," she said. "There are many hiding places and hundreds of kilometres of tunnels in these hills. Which art restorer?" she added.

"A Russian called Serge Piezenski. You might know him?"

"Everyone knows Serge Piezenski. He is a Bordeaux legend..." Marie-Joëlle's face became still in concentration.

"Ah, the forgery *scandale*," she said eventually. "That is the link."

"It would appear so. But back to the autopsy report..."

"It is very shocking to read the details," said Marie-Joëlle.

"Yes it is. Even with my imperfect French, it's a shock. I wonder if you would mind if I copied some details down?"

"Oh no, that is your copy to keep. We photocopied it for you to have. You do promise not to tell the police. I could not live with myself if anything happened to Cappucine."

"Sure, of course. It makes you wonder who this guy on the bike is. Some kind of police insider who trades stuff like this routinely for cash?"

"I think so. I think he knew I was staying with Cappucine and rightly thought I would be the highest bidder. You see I would have paid whatever he asked for that information." She ran her thumb and forefinger up and down the stem of her glass.

"I sometimes think that we are wrong to see the battle lines drawn between police and criminal. Actually they are close allies, feeding one on the other. The real war is between them on the one side and the rest of us on the other." With that Marie-Joëlle got up, pecked Starr on the cheek and left him with the bill and his thoughts.

Damien Refeuille was the killer, of that he was increasingly sure, in spite of his early misgivings. But did that mean his mother did just die of a heart attack and it was pure coincidence that the police arrived shortly afterwards? Was that likely? And there remained another mystery that would take a reply from Shawcross' new iPhone to unravel.

Starr found the scrap of paper on which Shawcross had scribbled his new number and set about texting him. He'd not get it until his plane reached Hong Kong but one night was nothing to wait in the grand scheme of things.

Back at La Borie, Starr settled down to finish his neglected movie theme crossword, the pink Champagne fuelling his creativity (or so he told himself) when the loud whirring blades of a helicopter disturbed his concentration. He strolled to the edge of his garden to see if he could spot it when it appeared overhead, hovered low over La Borie and then banked steeply, following the hillside that dipped down to the river. There followed the sound of a loud splitting, like a tree being felled, but Starr didn't realise its significance until he heard the sirens ten or fifteen minutes' later.

Starr drove down the vine-covered hillside to the lazy, grey Dordogne and followed her meandering course along the D670 west. Just before he came to the small town of Lugon et l'isle du Carnay he caught a glimpse of the Chateau de la Vielle Chapelle – a modest, square house parked right on the banks of the river as she curved away towards Bordeaux. The chateau made a decent wine and had a small *chambres d'hôtes* business. He'd stayed there a few times when Esmé and he were first house-hunting in the area. As he drove into the limestone *cour* a couple of English setters padded up to greet him, followed by the chatelaine herself.

"Bonjour Madame," he said. "It's Francine isn't it?"

"Yes it is – should I know you?"

"No, not at all. My wife and I stayed with you 12 or 13 years ago. There's no reason why you would remember."

"I'm sorry, Monsieur, we are all a little flustered by the *tragédie*, but actually I do remember you. You are from New York. You were buying a 'ouse."

"That's very impressive – you're absolutely right. I have a house now up at Sainte Croix. I'm here because I heard a crash, I think. Was it the helicopter?"

"You don't know? Yes, yes it was Monsieur Bloiseau. He was with the new buyer of his chateau: a Chinese hotelier, called Li Wok. It crashed just round the bend of the river. You can see the police boats from our terrace," she said, leading Starr to the place.

There you could see the mangled blades of the helicopter sticking out of the river at an angle and police arc lights mounted on the banks. There were uniformed gendarmes, two fire engines and police divers in the water.

"The Chateau de la Rivière?" Starr asked.

"They were making a tour of the area, to celebrate the sale," said Francine, shaking her head. "I believe they only signed the papers earlier this afternoon. Thomas, my 'usband, took the tractor to see if he could help. One of the chateau's vignerons from the chateau was there and he told him."

"Do you think they're dead?" Starr couldn't help but ask.

"Certainly we saw two bodies in bags so at least two people died. As for the rest, I don't know. Of course we locals cannot help thinking it's the chateau curse."

"Curse?"

"Well, the previous owner of Chateau de la Rivière before Monsieur Bloiseau, was killed in a plane crash ten years' ago, Monsieur."

"How strange," Starr shivered.

"Will you come in and have a glass of wine? My husband should be here in a minute. He's putting the chickens away for the night."

"*Avec plaisir*," said Starr and followed her to the mellow stone house with its white shutters and matching lemon trees in pots by the front door.

Starr was shown into the long, flagged salon, with shabby soft furnishings and a few old family portraits on the walls. A fire was blazing in the enormous inglenook. Starr flopped down in one of the sagging armchairs by the fire and flicked through the magazines that lay on a side table. With a lurch of his stomach he saw the previous month's issue of *Cuvée* and Sylvie's name against one of the cover lines.

He could hear husband and wife chatting, then the squat dark figure of Thomas appeared with a tray of glasses and an opened bottle. Some toasts with a duck terrine accompanied it.

Francine performed the introductions and then they all settled by the fire, a large glass of the chateau's fine '05 vintage in their hands.

"*Santé*," Thomas said.

"Francine was telling me that you were there on the scene before the police arrived?"

"*Ah oui, Monsieur.* I took the *tracteur* along to see if I could help pull it out, you know, but there was nothing to be done."

"Do you know who was on board?"

"Not really. Grégoire Bloiseau was *pilote* and there was the new owner, Li Wok, and his wife and teenage son, I believe. Someone from the chateau said that there was also an interpreter, but I don't know if that's true."

All three shook their heads and stared into the leaping flames of the fire, the comfort and safety of the room in stark contrast to the watery death outside. Starr felt glowing and guilty in almost equal measure, as he began to wonder how, if at all, this latest drama fitted with Sylvie's death.

As Starr drove the 20 minutes home, his cellphone beeped and checking it, he was surprised to see a reply to his message to Shawcross. Not only must the old rogue have worked out how to turn it on, but he must be using the plane's business class mobile service too. He turned the car into the side of the road, left his indicator on, and read the message.

"Cant remmembr her name but yes from DCF Paris. Detective specialist wine fraud. v. knwoddgeable. Natural blonde, I thhnk. JS"

It might take Jim a while to master the small touchscreen's keyboard, but the message was clear enough. The woman in the picture was none other than Christiane Montreux.

CHAPTER

10

naïs' flat in the rue des Faures was everything La Borie was not. The grand 18th century building was at the heart of Bordeaux's Saint-Michel quartier, and from its fifth floor vantage point it had views south to the Quai des Salinières, where salt to preserve fish was once loaded onto the quay from flat-bottomed boats on the Garonne. To the north was a squint view of the grand basilica of the archangel himself.

You entered the building through a door cut into a vast much bigger door and found yourself in a small, shady courtyard where the bustle of the bars and restaurants that filled the street were left behind. Clipped box boules in terracotta pots surrounded a small stone fountain. Fortunately there was a lift, although Anaïs, no doubt to show off her athleticism, liked to race Starr, who would stab the elevator button in competitive spirit, as she bounded up the spiralling shallow wooden staircase that united the ground floor all the way to the flats in the mansard roof on the 5th floor.

It was furnished in an eclectic selection of Scandinavian classics from the 1950s, some upcycled industrial furniture and other contemporary designer pieces from Bordeaux. There were statement artworks on the white walls. But tucked away in one corner was the one of Anaïs' possessions that caused Starr almost physical envy: a walnut tipping *table de vigneron*, with plain trestle legs, no more than a metre in diameter, simple and superb.

Starr was stretching in the large, low bed when Anaïs brought him coffee and croissants from the bakery on the corner of the street. She'd pulled on some track bottoms and a T-shirt over her warm, naked body just to dive in and out and was now undressing again, Starr was relieved to see.

"What time have you got to be in the gallery?"

"Not 'till later. They owe me for all these *vernissages*."

"Mmm, lucky me," he ran his hand down her narrow back and drew her body next to him.

Anaïs was unlike any of his previous lovers. When he tried to describe her, he resorted to cliché but the woman herself was far from cliché. She combined exoticism and sophistication in a way that seduced body and mind in equal measure. She had a confidence that filled Starr with awe: she would wander about the apartment naked, oblivious of the fact that the accountants and civil servants on the opposite side of the street had a prime view, and reprimand him for being bourgeois if he pointed this out. She had majored in Economics at MIT, and her approach to art was never sentimental. She applauded courage and individuality, and was acutely aware of the market – one that was spiralling upward for almost all the artists the gallery represented. His wife, Esmé, and he had been peas in a pod; they matched. He and Anaïs didn't match – they came from different planets, but mutual attraction had flickered like static over the gap between them and brought them here.

Anything Starr quite liked, she covered in scorn. "Derivative, cosy," were typical pejorative terms. It was the first time Starr had been in a relationship that he had not led. On only the second time they had met, she had suggested a drink at her apartment, and he, in his naivety, had thought 'drink' is what she meant. She made love as she lived: confidently, boldly, without hesitation. She had no difficulty in expressing her needs and pursuing the things that made her happy.

"The coffee's cold," Anaïs stretched langorously on top of the bed.

"I'll make a new pot," Starr offered and pulling on his boxers took the tray that Anaïs had prepared an hour before.

"I meant to tell you – you know Piezenski is back from Italy," she hollered through the open bedroom door.

Starr paused as he filled the cafetière with boiling water.

"The Russian restorer? How do you know?"

"I saw him yesterday. He was in 'Wine and Soul' with a couple of guys who looked like collectors."

"In the rue de Couvent?" Starr knew the place well, its glass brick walls and overpriced menu drawing in tourists and poseurs in equal numbers.

"Yes, it was definitely him."

Starr brought the tray of coffee back to the bed and they both started munching on the croissants, no longer really warm, but flaky and chewy in exactly the right combination.

"Would you come with me to his studio?" Starr asked through his full mouth.

"Will you what?" laughed Anaïs, imitating his food-muffled voice .

"Sorry. Would you come with me to Piezenski. I want to check him out but I need some ruse, some story."

"The easiest is to say you have a painting that needs work, make it up."

"Yeh, but I'm shit at the art-speak. Pleeeease come."

"Oh for Christ's sake, Franklin. OK but leave the talk to me."

"Thanks... I'll owe you. Anything you want."

"Really? Anything?" she raised her two curving eyebrows and flashed him a meaningful look.

A clock behind them struck 11, as Starr and Anaïs turned down the rue Ferrière to Piezenski's atelier. It had a huge glass frontage – not modern, but divided by 19th century wood frames – that gave passers-by intriguing tableaux of the interior that was filled with paintings of different sizes and eras; some propped on easels, others leaning against the walls. At the back was a large wood counter. They entered what seemed to be an empty shop.

Anaïs strode up to the counter and hollered *"Bonjour! Personne?"*

A small, thin man appeared silently through a side-door. He had close-cropped white hair and was wearing a striped shirt and dark green waistcoat over close-fitting narrow trousers. He was what you'd call dapper. His intensely blue eyes darted over the two of them like some kind of robotic laser storing the scanned information on its hard drive. He smiled, but did not speak.

"I wonder if you can help us," said Anaïs, smiling broadly. "I have inherited a painting from my great aunt that has hung in her house in Guadeloupe for decades and is in need of considerable restoration work."

"Guadeloupe?" said the nameless figure, quietly, with its strong East-European accent.

Anaïs opened her large brown eyes fringed by the thick, long lashes and nodded.

"It's a Gaughin," she said, "So you see we are anxious that it should be handled with care."

"Paul Gaughin," said the monosyllabic restorer, a wry, disbelieving smile curling his thin lips, "did not paint the Caribbean."

"Monsieur, please don't patronise me. I am quite aware of the artist's travels and subjects," said Anaïs. "The painting has been in the family for three generations and was gifted by the artist; it appears in all the major monographs and we have no doubt of its authenticity. But decades in a tropical climate hasn't done it any favours."

Starr tried to look as blank as possible but was watching the man he presumed to be Piezenski with interest.

"Authenticity," repeated the man. "You expect me to believe you are in possession of a Post-impressionist masterpiece and you just walk into my atelier, *sans rendez-vous*."

Anaïs looked unperturbed.

"If you're not interested in the job, just say. Ray Waterhouse recommended you."

"Ray Waterhouse from Sotheby's?"

"The very same. He's valued the piece for me, because frankly I don't much care to have four nipples in orange and green staring from my salon walls. He says the painting needs expert cleaning."

Starr noted how the Russian, for he was more and more sure this was Piezenski, was swallowing the bait. He made quick, fluttery gestures with his hands and his eyes burned with a bird-like greed about to stab a fat worm.

"We can, of course, do the work, but I will need to see it before giving you a *devis*. I should warn you we are also very busy and currently have a waiting list, so I hope there is no immediate urgency." He stared this time not at Anaïs but at Starr who did his best to stare back.

"Are you insured?" Anaïs asked.

"Insured, Madame?"

"Yes, against loss or damage."

Piezenski smiled. "Naturally," he said. "We handle work for the finest collectors and museums in the world. We are fully insured."

"Good," said Anaïs. "So what's the next step? Do I bring the painting here or are you able to visit me?"

"I can make a house call," he said. "Where do you reside?"

Starr's stomach lurched as he had visions of Piezenski and the Russian heavies he felt sure lurked behind the enigmatic side-door, turning up at rue des Faures and Anaïs bludgeoned on the floor.

"Les Trois Etoiles, Saint-Emilion," Starr broke in.

"Les Trois Etoiles, the bar?" Piezenski was not amused.

"Yeh, the little office above the bar," said Starr staring at him.

"You must leave," said Pienzenski. "You make a very serious mistake to play jokes with me. I have..." and he paused for effect, "connections. Now get out of my atelier."

And with that he made a sudden and threatening movement from behind the counter and Starr and Anaïs almost ran out of the shop and up the street before falling into each others' arms with mutual relief and laughter.

Starr lit a cigarette and realised his hands were trembling.

"Gaughin?" he blurted out.

"Yeh well it had to be something flashy to pique his interest and at least I know a bit about Gaughin. Anyway I think he'd bought it until you ruined it with Les Trois Etoiles!"

Starr put his long arm round the narrow shoulders of Anaïs Dugommier and together they strolled up the cobbled street near the quay, allowing their heart rates to slow gradually.

"I had to test him to see if it had a reaction," said Starr.

"Well, I think we can safely say affirmative to that."

"He knows Refeuille all right, and that has to mean he's doing the forging."

"Wine labels?"

"Shawcross said that in Hong Kong the dodgy wine had been a mix of genuine and very good forgeries, printed using old ink on Ingrès paper. This is the work of an expert. Someone who has access to records and to the pigments in use hundreds of years ago. Why else did Refeuille escape into Piezenski's atelier if not because he knew him?"

"The trouble now is Piezenski knows we know," said Anaïs. "Not only that...but...I have to go to work!"

Starr looked at his watch. It was 11.40am. "Take care," he said and kissed her.

"Don't forget you owe me," she said.

He stood and watched her walk up the narrow street, hips swaying, head held high, her large handbag clasped under one shoulder. She never looked back, not now, not ever.

Starr strolled to the small square behind Anaïs' apartment where he parked his car. It wasn't until he beeped the doors open that he noticed. All four tyres had been slashed and the car stood on its wheel rims. He looked around as if the idiots who'd done it were going to be lurking nearby. You couldn't even park your car in this hip, residential part of Bordeaux, he was thinking, without some mindless act of vandalism ruining your day. Walking round the car he saw, with a shiver, the word "Gaughin" written in the artist's familiar signature, the cursive letters each separated, in the grime of the rear window.

He dialled Dacour.

"Starr, why did you go to Piezenski's *atelier*? You must leave this to the police. I'll get the blame for this," he said bitterly.

"Hang on, Dacour. I'm trying to help, you know. And you don't seem to be doing any better. Did you know Refeuille visited his mother in the maison de retraite shortly before you found her body? Yeh? Did you?"

"How do you know this? Who told you this? When will you leave police work to the professionals?" Dacour was angry.

"Look I can tell you everything but I need you to give me a hand getting new tyres on my car. We're supposed to be on the same side," he added.

"OK," said the inspector decisively. "Place Gambetta, half an hour." He hung up and Starr hurried to a cramped little café on the opposite side of the square. He ordered a double espresso and sat near the back, fear coiling in his guts. This was the moment he knew that what had started as a quest for the truth, for absolution for all his many sins of omission, had now turned into something both dark and dangerous. Something told him he had crossed the line from adventure to nightmare. He was way out of his depth and worse, had dragged Anaïs in with him.

The police tow truck was punctual and efficient. It took the two *policiers* less than ten minutes to load his car and drive away while Dacour and he smoked cigarettes in silence in the leafy square now bustling with workers on their lunch hour.

"Can't you get a warrant to search Piezenski's place?" Starr finally spoke.

"I can't go near Refeuille or Piezenski. The Bordeaux branch of the DCF is investigating a major fraud now. The murder investigation has to be sensitive to this," Dacour said bleakly.

"Shall we get into your car? The wind's come up and it's getting cold," Starr shivered.

Soon they were snaking through the busy one-way system of central Bordeaux, crossing the tramlines, past the famous mirror fountain down to the vast grey Garonne. Starr was deliberating how much to share with Dacour. It wasn't that he mistrusted him, exactly, but he knew that he wasn't sharing everything; beneath the lined face and grey pallor secrets lay folded in manilla envelopes and plastic evidence bags. Was he aware of Christiane Montreux's real identity, for example? Did he know there was an informant selling police secrets? Who had removed Sylvie's mobile and then planted it in Refeuille's jacket pocket? No, he would prod a little, but not show his hand.

"Did you get anywhere with Madame Refeuille's glasses case?" Starr asked. Dacour put his foot on the gas as they got onto the motorway system driving east towards Libourne.

"There were no traces and just Madame Refeuille's fingerprints," said Dacour.

"But she was on prescription sleeping pills, wasn't she?"

"All the patients in Sainte Marie have prescriptions to help them sleep, Starr. It's routine."

"Hmm. But not everyone is on rohypnol," Starr chanced.

"Rohypnol?" Dacour played dumb under his poker face.

"Yes didn't you say something about rohypnol?"

"You know very well I have never mentioned it," said the inspector. "It is revealing that you have, though."

"Sorry, I thought it was you. It must have been one of the staff at the nursing home told me."

"Really? And what else did this mystery informant let you know?"

They were now driving fast over the wide river-bed of the Dordogne; the Mirabelles were all in bridal blossom and the blackened timber tobacco barns reminders of what had once dominated these warm, flat plains before the vines marched down from the hillsides and occupied them.

"I know Damien Refeuille visited regularly, every week, and that he was there the morning of Madame Refeuille's death. I also know that she was alive when he left, according to a cleaner who was tidying her room."

"Hmm. He could have doubled back, though?"

"I guess. But I thought you said there was nothing suspicious in her death anyway?"

"That was my initial perception."

Starr waited for him to enlarge, but when nothing but silence filled the car, he prompted,

"But now?"

"Now we have the results of the autopsy."

"Which means?"

"I have had to review my initial thought," he continued.

"So was she murdered?" Starr was impatient.

"I cannot discuss the case with you, Starr. You can draw your own conclusions. But I can confirm we are now investigating two suspicious deaths, which may, or may not, be related."

Starr was silent. Refeuille must have left his mother's room to ensure the cleaner provided him with an alibi and then, perhaps waiting outside the French doors, come back. What was his motive? Was she going to rat on her beloved son? According to Oriane they were mutually devoted, though.

"There is something else you may be interested to know. We found a set of keys in Refeuille's office in Saint-Emilion. Judging from the type and age of the keys, we think they must belong to an old building. We are looking for an 18th century lock to match the 18th century keys."

"Where have you tried so far?"

"Only Chateau Benedictus' chais. The chateau and the chais are the right period, but none of the locks fitted."

"Is de Bachelet a suspect?" Starr asked in disbelief. He couldn't quite see the suave aristocrat lowering himself to murder.

"Who knows? Everyone is a suspect. There are too many people who could have done it."

Starr didn't know why he thought what surfaced in his troubled mind at that moment.

"Do you know the Chateau de la Rivière?" he blurted out as they turned off the motorway to Libourne.

Dacour snatched a meaningful glance at his passenger.

"Why do you mention it?"

"Actually I'm not sure. But there was that terrible helicopter crash, and for some reason I think maybe the Chateau de la Rivière is caught up, entangled, in all this."

"We are working with the air accident authorities – there is no sign of, how do you say, malfeasance."

The detective seemed for a moment to have forgotten Starr was in the car and in minutes was speaking into his hands-free mobile.

"Oui, Michel. Chateau de la Rivière. Bring the keys. Yes of course in the bag. Oh and call them and – don't mention any particular crime – say we would much appreciate testing some keys that have been handed in. *Comment?*"

Starr tried to make out the muffled second half of this dialogue.

"No, we don't need a warrant. We are just trying to unite the keys with the locks. *Comprends?*"

Dacour had ignored the signs to 'centre ville' and was swinging though the series of roundabouts that enclosed the town. Soon they were bowling along the narrow road that led up towards the vine-covered flanks of the lazy Dordogne that unravelled herself langorously in her lush green bed below.

Chateau de la Rivière was a semi-fortified chateau with crenellated towers and high, four storied, walls. It stood in a commanding position dominating the landscape, its vineyards sweeping down beneath the chateau's paternal, watchful eye.

The police car had arrived before them and Michel and another uniformed *policier* were busy chatting with a chateau employee as the detective parked his car in the elegant driveway that fronted the house.

Dacour flashed his badge, introduced Starr as a police *expert*, and nodded to his two colleagues.

"Madame Margueron," the chateau representative, was a middle-aged woman, dressed in a navy blue suit, a Hermès scarf round her neck, professional, used to dealing with the public. "Keys, you say? We have had no break-ins, *Inpsecteur,* no. Just journalists coming to take photos and snoop around after the *tragedie,*" she shook her head.

"Commiserations," said Dacour. "It must have been a terrible shock for you all."

"They had only signed the *acte de vente* that afternoon," Madame Margueron continued.

"And the whole family of the Chinese buyers were in the helicopter?" Starr asked.

"*Mais non, Monsieur.* Li Wok's wife, Madame Changying, she stayed behind at the last minute, because she was too frightened to fly. Now she has the chateau to run and her husband and 12 year-old son to mourn."

Dacour flashed Starr a look that shut him up and the party of four followed Madame Margueron to the large limestone chais that lay to one side of the chateau.

"What makes you think the keys belong here?" asked Madame Margueron as they walked.

"No particular reason," said Dacour truthfully. "We are working through a list of chateaux in the region with 18th century chais. We know the keys belong to that period and many chateaux have long since changed their locks. It is an outside chance but we are grateful for your time. We can at least eliminate Chateau de la Rivière."

"You must have a long list," she said.

Starr could see that the large wooden doors of the first chai had a system of five-lever locks that were modern and recently installed. Madame Margueron unlocked the door and flicked the chai lights illuminating the light oak barrels that stretched as far as the eye could see in every direction.

"When the chateau refurbished its chais in 2008," Madame Margueron said, "the locks were changed. You will not find what you are looking for here."

Starr lurked behind as the rest of the party marched briskly up and down the aisles towards the back of the vast stone wine barn that led into the chateau's second enormous chai. Through the doorway you could see the chateau's second growth vintages, maturing in steel vats. Starr remembered Shawcross telling him that most chateaux had internal passageways that gave direct access from the chateau building to the chais, often dug into the limestone and he wondered idly if such a passage existed here. He was exploring the wall adjacent to the chateau when without warning the chai was plunged into extreme darkness, the only light the small, distant doorway that led into the second chai where Dacour and the rest of the group were forging ahead. Starr's heart throbbed in his ribcage. He pulled out his iPhone and fumbling to turn it on, found the torch app. The beam was reassuringly bright. He followed the ancient limestone wall looking for a doorway when the ice-white beam of his phone lit up a small rusty iron ring set into the floor in front of him. The flagstone around it looked just like all the others but on closer inspection, under the ring was a lock, an old lock. Starr hollered to Dacour and soon the chai was again flooded with light.

Starr pointed to the lock in the floor and the inspector shouted at Michel to bring the bag with the keys. Pulling on a pair of latex gloves and squatting down on the floor, Dacour tried each of the five keys in the hidden lock. On the third attempt, the sound of the old levers turning and eventually shooting the bolt echoed through the silent stone chai. Michel's bigger colleague heaved on the iron ring to open what was a stone trap door revealing a set of steps that led down into the blackness.

In the excitement, no-one noticed Madame Margueron leave.

They could find no light switch so Starr shone his phone beam down the rough-hewn steps and Dacour was first to ease himself down, his body throwing a long shadow in front of him like some neolithic human form flickering on the uneven walls.

"Give me the phone, Starr," he said.

The policemen hovered at the entrance to the stairway, so Starr suggested that he follow Dacour and they stay and stand guard. His heart still thumping, he bent his long body into the tiny space and crouching his head followed the figure of the policeman.

The tunnel was hand-carved out of the rock, and Starr had to crouch to avoid banging his head. The steps curved in a sharp bend before stopping in a small series of underground caverns. The air was moist and cool – ideal for keeping wine. There were some very old small oak wine barrels – some decrepit and broken, others intact – and a store of carefully organised empty bottles.

"You there, Starr?" Dacour half-whispered.

"Just behind you. What have you found?"

"Take a look at this, but don't mention it when we go up. I'm going to take photos," he said, using the camera on Starr's phone.

There in the next small chamber was a table and two chairs, some powerful overhead lights and in boxes thousands of wine labels, some distressed, some apparently new. As Dacour busied himself with the photos, Starr surreptitiously grabbed a few examples of as many of the labels as he could reach without Dacour seeing and stuffed them into his coat pocket.

There were voices coming from the tunnel ahead followed by blinding light as the whole system of tunnels and caverns was illuminated and there in front of them, their long shadows spreading in front of them like dark bloodstains, were Christiane Montreux and Madame Margueron.

CHAPTER

11

"How long have you known that Christiane was from the DCF?" The detective was slumped uncomfortably on too small a little bistro chair, his espresso steaming in the afternoon sun.

"Only a few days," said Starr honestly, "I saw a photo of some investigation into an auction lot in Beijing. She was blonde but there was something I kinda half-recognised. Long before that though, I thought there was something a bit odd about her."

"Odd?"

"Well she told me about Sylvie's mobile phone being removed from the police evidence bag, before it was recovered in Refeuille's pocket. And I couldn't quite figure out why she confided in me."

"Maybe she liked you?"

"Ha! Yeh right."

The two men took long, synchronised, drags on their cigarettes and allowed their thoughts to run off, like gambolling dogs, in the silence.

"While I'm in the mood for confessionals, there's another theft you should know about – and a puzzle."

The crumpled detective raised his small, intent eyes and Starr felt again the uncomfortable sense of guilt, of being found out.

He told Dacour about the autopsy report and his mysterious text message that summoned him to the Maison de Retraite.

"May I see this message?"

Starr scrolled through his message list, clicked on the text and passed his phone for Dacour's forensic examination. Dacour tapped the number into his own phone and as Starr had found out himself, got an unobtainable signal. "Dead SIM."

"That's why you knew about the rohypnol," the detective continued.

Starr nodded, wondering why he seemed unsurprised that there was clearly a police leak.

"Mademoiselle Janneau's murder is just a small part of something much bigger," said Dacour. "I wish we'd have had longer in that cellar before the fraud boys sealed it off."

Starr slipped a hand into his jacket pocket and felt the stash of wine labels he had stuffed in there.

"You've changed your mind about Refeuille," Starr said more than asked.

The detective looked at him with his grey, impassive eyes.

"Not at all. Refeuille had means – his mother's rohypnol – motive – he is involved in a major wine fraud – and opportunity – he was the last to see Mademoiselle Janneau alive. He has a connection with Monsieur Piezenski who, I am sure, has been forging wine labels. But he cannot have operated alone. He has an accomplice – possibly a handler – someone who is working his strings. The question is, who is the puppet-master?"

"You're convinced Sylvie died because of this wine fraud – you've ruled out anything more personal, to do with her private life?"

Dacour was silent for a few seconds, apparently deciding how much of his thought processes to share with the persistent American.

"At the beginning I felt the *aventure* with Madame de Cazaux held the motive for the murder," Dacour spoke slowly. "A very powerful woman, a lesbian passion, and a husband, a prominent Paris publisher, who had been cheated on. Yes, I felt those were the elements we had to focus on..." his voice trailed off.

"Whereas now?" prompted Starr.

"Now I believe I was seduced by that power, by the colour of Mademoiselle's story. I no longer think these are crimes of the heart, even calculated crimes of the heart. These are crimes of the head."

"Did *Cuvée*'s wine editor – Valentin Somebody – did he have an alibi?"

"Yes. He was at the Envers de Décor, hosting a dinner with ten négociants, cavistes and chateaux owners, all of whom vouch for him. The party didn't leave until 2am, and the hotel desk remembered him coming back. He had difficulty using his card key so one of the room service waiters was called to help him. He couldn't have done it."

"Oh," Starr said absent-mindedly.

"He did leave the dinner but only for a few minutes to fetch a wine catalogue from his car. The caviste of Pavie had asked to see it and he produced it as evidence. Anyway the maitre d' at L'Envers said he left at about 11pm. Mademoiselle Janneau was still finishing her dinner date with Monsieur Refeuille when Monsieur Charpentier went to his car. It doesn't fit the timings and he would have had to abduct Mademoiselle Janneau, walk her to the Grandes Murailles, find the rope, tie her neck, forge the note and plant it in her handbag all within just a few minutes. Not possible. Anyway what would be his motive?"

"Professional jealousy?" Starr took a swig of the thick, strong coffee. "Why do you think they chose to hang Sylvie, and in such a kind of public place?"

The detective shrugged his rounded shoulders and said "Why not?"

"If it was just a question of getting Sylvie out of the way, of shutting her up, they could have, I don't know – strangled her or stabbed her and dumped the body in the countryside. Why dress it up as suicide?"

"Stabbing is not a good choice for murder," said Dacour in a matter-of-fact tone. "Too much blood, the potential for cries. Strangling is better but you have to know how to do it. This staged suicide was very well done; we were all taken in."

"Well not quite all," Starr said.

"You didn't want to believe it, that's true. But your emotions were involved. If you hadn't known the *victime* you would have accepted it as everyone else did."

Starr thought for a moment. Was that true? Did the killer assume a routine investigation would not really investigate below the surface, below what appeared to be the case. Was it Starr's determined refusal to believe Sylvie had taken, could take, her own life that had got him to contact LeBlond? Undoubtedly it played a part; plus the phoney note. That was so obviously a fake.

"I suppose we all see what we want to see, to an extent," Starr said eventually.

"The first being we meet in our ontological inquiry is the being of the appearance,'" quoted Dacour in French.

"Jean-Paul Sartre? I didn't mark you down as a philosopher, Dacour."

"You know nothing about me," replied the inspector wearily. "I studied *Philosophie* at the Sorbonne, before becoming *policier.*"

"Seriously? That's a strange path to the law."

"We follow different routes, but to the same destination," said the detective.

"'Truth is one, paths are many', as Gandhi said."

Dacour almost smiled before heaving his frame off its small iron perch, flinging a few coins on the terrace table and with a cursory *"à bientôt!"* he had gone up the cobbled hill to pursue his quest.

Starr decided to drive the long route home, up along the D245 northwest through the Saint-Emilion elite vineyards that nestled together just before the appelation gave way to Figeac. Here the wrought iron gates of Cheval Blanc kept the gawpers at bay. Starr slowed the car to see the immaculate rows of vines reaching right up to the chateau's gravel parking. Next to the square honeyed stone original house you could see the space-age new chai with its white wave of concrete sweeping to the ground and on the side the flight of shallow steps that led up to its extraordinary roof garden with views over the whole of Saint-Emilion and nearby Figeac. One of the chateau employees was showing round a small group of Chinese businessmen and their wives. No doubt they would be taken down to see the new age cement vats; a single vat for each small parcel of vines so that the unique characteristics of the terroir, be it gravel, sand or clay, are contained and concentrated. Cheval Blanc gleamed in the late spring sunshine, like the movie star it was, not a hair out of place and in full make-up.

As he dropped down the escarpment he took a left rather than the right that led to Sainte Croix and doubled back towards Saint-Emilion and the long gravel driveway to Chateau Benedictus, its marine pines throwing deep pools of midnight blue shadow in symmetrical patterns as he drove the old Peugeot through them.

De Bachelet was to be found in his library – an elegant, but relatively modest room filled, of course, from floor to ceiling with fitted rosewood shelving housing his family's considerable book collection. A fire was blazing in the hearth. The aristocrat himself was quietly sitting at his partner desk, its tooled leather surface filled with orderly objects, arranged methodically.

As his housekeeper showed Starr in, he rose from the desk, placed his half-moon wire-rimmed glasses carefully on his desk and smiled warmly.

"This is a nice surprise," he said. "You've rescued me from my weekly accounts."

"Tell me if this is a bad moment," said Starr. "I was just passing."

"Never a bad moment," said de Bachelet graciously. "You are always welcome at Benedictus, you know that."

He motioned to the housekeeper who was discreetly hovering in the hallway beyond the library door and mimed drinking from a cup. The coffee came in two large Sèvres cups with a bowl of brown sugar cubes and cream in a small silver jug with a peach-skin fuzz of condensation.

The chateau owner and Starr settled in matching leather chairs, cupping the steaming coffee and separated by common thoughts.

"So?" asked de Bachelet, raising his eyebrows in enquiry.

"I don't know really," replied Starr to the unspoken question. "I feel that I'm been given the runaround, but can't put my finger on it. No-one is quite being honest – even that detective Dacour – and yet superficially it seems obvious that Refeuille is Sylvie's killer."

De Bachelet was silent.

"Perhaps we should just accept that sometimes the obvious is nevertheless the truth," de Bachelet pronounced.

"I can't. There's something all too neat about it and I don't believe Refeuille would murder his mother. Doesn't fit."

"This is not our *métier*," said the venerable wine-grower. "Leave it to the police and get on with life."

Starr ignored him and continued, "There's a wine fraud here – big scale wine fraud. And Sylvie fell into it and paid with her life."

"Monsieur Starr," sighed de Bachelet. "There have always been some unscrupulous négociants who may occasionally be less than extra-virgin in their transactions. You should not assume that the whole industry is dishonest. There are now many safeguards – individually etched bottles, complete traceability of wine back to the vine. It is not possible to fake the *grands cuvées* any longer."

De Bachelet carefully placed his cup on its wide saucer.

"That doesn't stop older wine from being faked, though, before all this high tech stuff came in. I don't know. You start to think everyone's involved after a bit," Starr shook his head. "Even you."

De Bachelet raised an aristocratic eyebrow but looked amused rather than affronted.

"The reputation of a great wine takes many different elements to achieve," he said. "The terroir, the tending of the vines, the weather – that's God's work – the expert blending and maturation. But we must not forget there is also communication, branding. What you Americans call marketing. These are relatively new skills that today's chateau owner must master." De Bachelet looked into the fire that crackled in the 18th century hearth. "Everything has a price in this world. Even the reputation of a great wine."

"You mean paying for a reputation? I'd call that bribery!"

"That is an ugly word. I prefer to think of it as paying for a service. You are going to pay anyway. It is just a question of to whom and when."

"That's just weak. If everyone thought like that, the world would be one big lie."

"Not a lie, perhaps," said de Bachelet. "More a version of the truth. You tell your story. Everyone tells their story."

Starr was silenced by the pounding of his head as he tried to factor in the implications of de Bachelet's words.

"Take the case of La Marzelle," de Bachelet continued. "The chateau lost its premier grand cru classé status in the last classification and perhaps the reason it lost it was not the quality of its wine, but a refusal to recognise how the wine market works today. I am not saying this is the case. Just that it is possible."

De Bachelet's implication that chateaux were paying for classifications had long been rumoured. The impunity of the crimson-robed Jurade had been called into question by media reports and at least two high-profile books. But, thought Starr, Jim Shawcross had always dismissed the rumours as sour grapes in a system that had losers as well as winners.

"And of course, it is not only the classification that matters to a wine's reputation, to its price," continued de Bachelet. "Your compatriot Mr Parker is a very large factor – as are other prominent wine writers' views. This is what happens when making wine is no longer an art, a tradition, when it becomes a business," de Bachelet did not hide his revulsion for the word.

"You mean wine reviews and writers? Yeah I get that. But hanging someone? I can't see the leap from wanting to influence to murder. It's too long a stretch."

"Perhaps she stepped into a *nid de guêpes* – a hornets' nest," said de Bachelet and the phrase reminded Starr of his own hornets and the odd man covered head to toe in protective overalls who had arrived to destroy them.

Starr shivered and saw an opportunity to change the subject.

"I heard you've had your own spot of insect trouble here at Benedictus."

"You mean the termites in our chaix? Yes, we've had to have the whole roof treated. You can't take any chances with termites; they can destroy whole streets you know," the aristocrat paused abruptly.

"Actually that reminds me. A strange thing happened. The how-do-you-say, 'operatives', disposed of their overalls and masks in the refuse bins in our *cour*, but Philippe noticed that they'd been removed just a few days later. *Bizarre, n'est ce pas?*"

Starr again felt something snap in his brain, but he wasn't sure why. A short silence followed as the two men explored their private thoughts.

"Anaïs – err, a friend of mine – she said that perhaps Sylvie was killed as a message, a warning."

"A perceptive remark. Sylvie Janneau was, perhaps, the *amiral tué pour encourager les autres*," de Bachelet quoted the famous line from Voltaire's *Candide*.

"Killed to encourage the others, yes," mused Starr. "But what others? You know that Damien Refeuille's mother was killed?"

"Yes I had heard that. Unfortunate certainly," he said.

"In fact it was when you were there, playing the piano."

"A coincidence," de Bachelet did not appear ruffled by the implication.

"I mean it's one thing slipping a few thousand euros to the Jurade," continued Starr. "It's quite another murdering old ladies in their beds."

"I couldn't agree more. They are not the same at all."

"Am I missing something?" Starr persisted.

De Bachelet stared into the leaping flames of his wood fire.

"You might want to think a little of the safety of those you love," he said finally. "There are ruthless men in this little world of ours who have far too much to lose to allow a meddling American to..." his voice trailed off. "Just be careful, Starr. You – we – are in danger, I believe. Leave it to the authorities. The police. You will not win this particular battle."

As Starr drove back up the pine-lined driveway, out through the stone pillars, he reflected on what had just happened. De Bachelet hadn't denied offering bribes in return for favourable wine reviews but it flew in the face of what Starr felt he knew of this man. He was so old school, so beyond reproach and so steeped in his family's traditions and reputation. Was de Bachelet really frightened both for himself and for Starr or was he acting to try to put Starr off? Did that mean Starr was getting close?

The phone was ringing from the depths of La Borie as he turned his key in the back door lock.

"*Allo*," he gasped breathlessly.

"Monsieur Starr, are you alright?" It was Christiane Montreux. She had not been in touch since the discovery of the forged wine labels in the tunnels under the Chateau de la Rivière.

"Sorry, I was just coming into the house. Had to run for the phone. What's up?"

"What's up is a body has just been taken out of the river in Bordeaux," she said. "And I thought you might like to know."

"Body? Who is it?"

"Damien Refeuille," she said the name tenderly, as though she knew him. "He has drowned. Discovered by some students still suffering from a little too much good wine the night before. His body was found at the quai du Paludate."

"Was he...killed?" Starr was still trying to take in the news.

"We won't know for certain until the autopsy, but it looks like suicide or misadventure. There is a bruise on his head, but that might just be where he fell into the water. I just called because I thought you would like to know."

"Sure," said Starr.

"Perhaps justice has been done, after all," she said.

"You mean an eye for an eye."

"*Précisement.* I also called because I will soon be returning to Paris."

"Oh really? The wine matter is finished: you have your culprits?"

"We have concluded that Damien Refeuille was working on his own, perhaps with the aid of a master-forger, perhaps alone. He had successfully put some counterfeit wine into some major auctions in Hong Kong and the Far East, but the project was relatively small-scale. And now...well he is dead, so there is no more to do."

"What about Piezenski? Isn't he involved?"

"There is no evidence to support that theory and although there have been several press stories, there is nothing behind the smoke. I have interviewed Monsieur Piezenski extensively and searched his premises. Nothing to link him to counterfeit operations."

"And what about the murder investigations? Are they closed too?"

"You will have to ask Inspecteur Dacour but it is my understanding that the Procureur is satisfied that Refeuille was guilty of both murders so no further investigations may be necessary. Of course that assumes the autopsy confirms no sign of, what is the English phrase? Ah yes, foul play. Anyway, I enjoyed meeting you, and our trip to the Cercle Rive Droite. Go carefully, Monsieur Starr," and with that she hung up.

Starr stood looking at the phone. Case closed. He poured himself a glass of wine that was open in the fridge and was about to take it onto the terrace when the phone rang again.

"Starr."

There was a silence of perhaps three seconds.

"It's Dacour. Refeuille has been found drowned in Bordeaux," he said finally.

"Yes I've just heard. Christiane Montreux called to let me know."

"Ah *vraiment,* she called you? She was there to identify the body, there being no immediate family any longer. I think it upset her. You don't see many bodies in the fraud division," that familiar smirk in his voice.

"Was it murder?" asked Starr, struggling to see the cool Christiane having any difficulty with the sight of a corpse.

"Nothing to suggest violence," said the inspector. "I'm seeing the Procureur with the crime file later and of course we have to wait for the autopsy results but it looks as though we have reached the end of the inquiry."

"Case closed," said Starr with little conviction.

"Apparently, yes," said Dacour and hung up abruptly.

This is where the final theme plays and the credits roll, Starr thought. Why do I feel no sense of an ending? Refeuille had means, opportunity and motive. He was filling old bottles with new wine and passing it off. He had the connections to make that a lucrative business. He stole rohypnol from his mother and laced Sylvie's wine so that she became unsteady and easy to control. He could then walk her to the edge of the town, string her up with little effective resistance and kick away the wine crates. There would be few people braving that cold March air at night. Sylvie threatened to blow the lid off his scam. But why kill his own mother? Would she really have told the authorities about the rohypnol?

Starr felt for his little wine tasting notebook and once again took it out. Methodically he listed the names of all the suspects. Then on the facing page he wrote a series of questions.

Who had forged the suicide note? Who had removed her cellphone from the scene and then planted it in Refeuille's pocket? Who had sent him the text to go to the Maison de Retraite and why? Why did de

Bachelet echo Anaïs' thought that Sylvie's death was a warning? Who was being warned and why? Who had stolen the autopsy report and sold it to Marie-Joëlle? What about the helicopter crash? Was that just coincidence too? There were too many unanswered questions, too much that made no sense.

Starr looked across his stretch of grass to the little row of now sprouting vines. It seemed months, years even, since he had pruned them with Anaïs looking on, her ironic smile lighting up her warm, open face. Beyond, the hillsides swept up into the clear sky, vines as far as the eye could see in every direction. Here and there a figure was bending performing some careful procedure, like tiny model figures in the vast landscape.

Then he had an idea and strode off to the low stone wall that marked the boundary between La Borie and the neighbour's vineyard. He waited for his iPhone to register two bars and dialled. Amazingly LeBlond answered the call.

"Bruno? Starr."

"One moment. I am just closing my office door. OK now. *Comment ça va?*"

"Bruno, they've found Refeuille's body floating in the Garonne."

"Ahh," said the eminent graphologist.

"What does 'ahh' mean?" Starr felt irritated. "Unless the autopsy shows signs of violence they'll close the case. All neat and tidy."

"And this is a problem because?"

"Because I don't believe Refeuille is in this alone. Did you hear about the discovery of forged labels found at Chateau de la Rivière?"

"Yes I did hear about that."

"You said yourself the forged suicide note was the work of an expert. How could a small-time négociant have done that?"

"It is not impossible to be both a négociant and a forger, *mon ami*."

"OK, maybe not. But what about being able to source the right paper, glues and inks to forge pre-1972 wine labels? The labels were such good forgeries that they fooled the greatest wine auctioneers in the world."

"I agree, from reading the press reports, nothing more you understand, that the wine labels discovered in Chateau de la Rivière were of an exceptional standard and that would require some very specialist knowledge that would, in normal circumstances, be outside the skillset of anyone not professionally involved in the study and restoration of fine art."

Starr smiled at Le Blond's correct, academic utterances; his fastidiousness.

"I have some of those wine labels," he said.

"From Chateau de la Rivière?"

"I was there when they were discovered and grabbed a handful at random."

"Where are they now?"

"Why here in my pocket," said Starr. "Do you want to see them?"

"No, no," replied Le Blond quickly. "I am a graphologist, nothing more. How many people know you have them?"

"Two. Me and now you."

"That's it? Are you sure?"

"Sure I'm sure. Why?"

"Perhaps you should put them somewhere very safe, *mon ami*. I cannot help you but there is a *laboratoire* in Pessac that specialises..."

"Yeh," cut in Starr. "I know about the Pessac lab. I was going to see it a while back, but things got in the way. But I know someone from the DCF; that police-woman is actually here for the wine fraud. I could show them to her?"

"No, no," said Le Blond. "I wouldn't do that. I suggest you tell no-one, really no-one, that you are in possession of these labels. I can telephone to the laboratoire and arrange a *rendez-vous* for you. You should go alone. Would that be helpful?"

Starr shivered. There was an urgency in Le Blond's voice that was uncharacteristic and faintly alarming.

"OK, if you think that's the best thing to do."

There was a short silence.

"Yes, I do. I will make the call and text you the details. *A bientôt* and go carefully," he said.

That was the second time someone had urged Starr to go carefully in the space of an hour. He returned to the terrace and took a gulp of the fine white Bordeaux that tasted of lemons and flint; there wasn't a hint of floweriness or fragrance. A suitably monkish wine, thought Starr, waiting for the ping that would tell him he had a text message.

"Tuesday, 11am, Lab SCL. Hélène Lafarge. Bonne chance, Bruno."

Starr had two more calls to make. First, he dialled Shawcross and got the voicemail.

He was luckier with the second call.

"I was beginning to feel neglected." Anaïs' voice filled Starr with reassurance.

"Can I come over tonight? Let's have dinner; you choose a place."

"You sound tired. Is everything OK?" she asked.

"Yeah, it's fine. I'll tell you everything when we meet."

"Sure. I'll be home by about 6.30pm. See you then – oh Franklin!"

"Yeah?"

"Guess who came to the gallery last night?"

"Surprise me."

"The great Piezenski himself. Plus two heavies."

Starr's stomach lurched and for a minute he couldn't speak. When he did, his voice sounded thin, strangled.

"Oh Christ, Anaïs. What did he want?"

"I think he wanted just to make his presence known. He looked round the new Jean-Georges Moulin show and then he left. He gives me the creeps though."

"Anaïs, promise me you will be careful. Don't open the apartment door to anyone, watch your back."

"Hey Franklin, this is me. I've nothing to fear from these guys. See you tonight," and she hung up.

Starr felt again the familiar dread coiling in his guts. A shower and a change would be good, he thought, and took the creaking wood stairs up three at a time.

The hot water was pounding on his head and over his bony shoulders with the force of a tropical storm when he thought he heard a creak on the stairs. He ducked his head out of the water to listen, without turning off the shower. Then he blacked out.

CHAPTER

12

Starr opened one eye and squinted at the stone flags that pressed against his cheek and jaw. He tried to move his head but quickly gave up. The shower was still pelting water somewhere beyond his right foot. He swivelled his eye to try to see more of the room and listened for sounds of his attacker. He could hear nothing beyond the shower that seemed unnaturally loud. He moved his legs in a scissor motion as the pain in his left knee shot up through his upper thigh. His lip tasted of blood. He had to get up, and damn the pain, he thought.

It took him what seemed like an age, hours perhaps. Every time he moved, something hurt or bled or both. The worst was the back of his head where he could feel a soft patch beneath the matted blood-soaked hair and any movement resulted in a wave of nausea and the threat of blacking out. He'd managed to reach for his abandoned T-shirt and had tied it in a kind of turban round the bloody wound. Eventually he made it to a crawl position, his left knee stretched out, taking no weight and in tiny, ginger movements, half-crawled, half-pulled himself along the narrow landing to his bedroom beyond.

It was a mess. Drawers were pulled out and emptied on the floor. His mattress was off the bed. Someone had done a thorough job. His jacket, left hanging on a chair, was gone and with it, he presumed, his mobile and wallet. Fuck, he thought, and collapsed onto the floor, blacking out again.

The next moment, it seemed, he awoke in Libourne Hospital. Sun was streaming through the half-open Venetian blinds, the institutional pale green on the walls and the stink of disinfectant and floor polish unmistakable hallmarks of hospitals the world over. Glancing down he saw that his left leg was entirely encased in plaster and was in a hoist above the bed and his head and jaw were bandaged, leaving just his face exposed. His left arm was connected up to a drip that had two bags. Saline and morphine he thought. He was alone in the two-bed room.

"*Ah Monsieur Starr, bonjour!*" The nurse was brusque and efficient. "Can I get you some tea?"

Starr grimaced.

"Coffee?"

He nodded and managed a "merci," before asking, "How long have I been here?"

"Since 11pm last night, Monsieur. A man who has been working on your house found you and telephoned the emergency services," she said brightly.

"Monsieur Acrylic Jumper!" said Starr to his uncomprehending attendant.

"You were fortunate he did," she said. "You had lost a lot of blood. But the doctor will be coming to see you and he will explain. You have had surgery on your knee and head."

The coffee arrived in a plastic beaker with a lid and a drinking spout, like children have. It was neither hot nor strong but it was good to be drinking something, anything.

The first visitor was not the doctor, however, but Dacour.

"You look terrible," he said impassively.

"Thanks. How did you know I was here?"

"The *pompiers* called us. Someone's done your house over, Starr. Upstairs is really a mess."

"Yes I saw that," said Starr, about to ask about the wine labels when Le Blond's warning words stopped him in his tracks. "I was in the shower."

Dacour pulled up a plastic visitor chair and got out a notebook.

"Are you up to a few questions?" he asked in his inspector voice. It was only then that Starr noticed that Michel, Dacour's No 2, was in uniform at the door.

"Yes I think so," he said.

"Tell me from the beginning what happened."

Starr explained that he had arranged to see a friend in Bordeaux for dinner, was in the shower and about to change when he heard someone on the stairs. He'd woken up on the floor, the shower still going and had with great difficulty half-crawled to his bedroom where he saw it had been ransacked. He remembered nothing after that.

"Name of friend in Bordeaux," said Dacour.

"Anaïs Dugommier. Apartment 5, 17 rue des Faures," he said. "Can you call her? She'll be worried. She works at MLS, the gallery."

The inspector wrote in his notebook in his copperplate, looping handwriting.

"Yes we will call her, but first, what had happened before you took the shower. Who had you called? Who had you met?"

"Err. No-one really. After you left me in the café I drove to Chateau Benedictus and had a coffee with Monsieur de Bachelet. Then I came home and got the call from Christiane Montreux about Damien Refeuille's body. Then you called with the same piece of news. I called Anaïs to suggest dinner tonight. *Fin.*"

"Why did you go to Chateau Benedictus?" asked Dacour.

"No particular reason. Monsieur de Bachelet is a friend of sorts, and it was almost on my way home."

"I would disagree," said Dacour. "It is quite a different direction from Sainte Croix."

"OK, but I felt like a drive and it was just a spontaneous decision, nothing more."

"Did you discuss the murder case with Monsieur de Bachelet?" pursued Dacour.

"Oh I don't know. Maybe a little. Not in any detail." Starr was finding the French detective's questioning increasingly irksome when he was saved by the appearance of three doctors in white coats, one clearly the main man with two matching acolytes.

The senior doctor barked at Dacour and chewed his ear for questioning his patient. Dacour smirked and said he'd be back later to finish his questions but in the meantime would visit Mademoiselle Dugommier in person.

The doctor checked the notes at the base of Starr's bed and then sat in the chair vacated by the detective.

"How is your memory?" he asked.

"How do you mean, in general or of the attack?"

"Let's start with the attack."

"Oh well I remember being in the shower, hearing someone on the stairs then blacking out. I awoke on the bathroom floor. I managed to half crawl into my bedroom with a T-shirt round my head but I must then have blacked out again. That's it until I woke up here."

The doctor nodded.

"And what day of the week is it?"

"Oh err Tuesday," and it was then Starr remembered his meeting at the Pessac lab, foiled again.

"And the President of France?"

"Emmanuel Macron, En Marche."

The doctor smiled.

"How many fingers am I holding up?"

"Three."

"Good. You have been fortunate Monsieur Starr. You were hit from behind with something blunt but heavy and it cracked your skull. There was some hematoma, bleeding, and we found a small piece of bone that just missed the cerebellum at the base of the skull. The outcome might have been very different if the blow had been a few millimetres to the side or if you had not been discovered until this morning."

"What about the leg?" asked Starr.

"Leg? Oh yes you have a fractured knee, probably as a result of your fall onto stone *tomettes*. I did not operate on your knee but it should cause no major problems. I think you will walk again. Eventually," he smiled benignly and Starr wasn't sure whether he was joking or not until he saw the obsequious grins on the faces of the two young side-kicks.

"How long will I be here?" asked Starr.

"That I can't tell you. The brain needs to heal and settle and the veins repair. Certainly a week, I would say, possibly longer. But you have made a good recovering after the surgery and we will not keep you longer than necessary. That I promise."

And with that, he swept out of the ward, his two novices following him like obedient spaniels.

Starr wanted to call the Pessac lab but he was going to follow Le Blond's advice and tell no-one about the labels, not even Dacour. Someone knew he had those labels, but who and how? Thank Christ, he thought, that he'd rolled them up and stashed them inside his trombone, almost on a whim, before he'd showered. They were still safe in his loft, he smiled, drifting off again into sleep.

"How long have you been here?" Starr asked, squinting through one half-opened eye.

Anaïs ignored the question and taking his hand, said, "You could have been killed, you know."

Starr grimaced in acknowledgment.

"Do you know what they were looking for? What they wanted?"

"Probably my tasting notes. They're priceless you know."

"Franklin darling, this is no longer a joke, a little amateur challenge. This is serious shit. Do you know that you've got a police guard on your hospital room?"

"Yeh, I saw the portly figure of the lovely Michel. The archangel himself! Who could ask for a better guardian angel?"

"Hey, I'm serious. This is a warning to back off. And that's what you're going to do. No more amateur sleuthing; no more visits to Piezenski; no more playing with fire."

"Did Dacour give you the news?"

"Huh? Yeah. He found me at the gallery, but I knew last night something bad had happened to you. You're never late and your cell went straight to voicemail. I would have driven over to La Borie but we had an early evening reception and I'd had a few, so I thought I'd be sensible."

"They took my cell," said Starr superfluously.

"You've seriously annoyed Dacour," Anaïs' mouth broke into a wide, generous smile.

"Oh yeah?"

"He says the whole Refeuille case was to have been closed today but your attack means the Procureur will probably defer a verdict until they find out who raided your house and why. He seemed to think I knew something; he was very insistent."

"Ignorance is bliss. Have they got police at the house?" Starr suddenly became anxious.

"Err, I don't know. Do you want me to ask Dacour?"

"Yeh, phone him now."

"Number?"

"Ah, damn, no phone. Try Michel and just say it's important."

Anaïs, who was wearing a rust-coloured dress and heels, swept out of the room and Starr heard her soft, deep voice through the closed door.

She was back in minutes, holding her cellphone to Starr's ear through the bandage.

"We have a police cordon," Dacour sounded impatient. "And forensics were there this morning for fingerprints. Perhaps you can tell me what they were looking for?"

Starr checked himself again.

"I really have no idea but now they have my cellphone, they'll have access to all my texts and contacts. I can't think who would want those though. No idea. I just think maybe the house should be guarded. I mean in case they come back."

Starr heard Dacour sigh at the other end of the phone.

"I can't commit our limited resources without a reason," he said deliberately. "And since you will not offer me a reason, no guard."

Starr then had an idea. "Capitaine, if Anaïs Dugommier drove over to La Borie, could she just collect my trombone from the house? Would that be OK? I am going to be so bored here and at least I could use the time to practise a bit."

"Trombone?" Dacour and Anaïs said almost in unison.

"Yeah. Brass instrument beloved of jazz musicians. I once played it almost well."

"OK, OK," Dacour said impatiently and hung up.

"You seriously want to play the trombone here?" Anaïs' smooth brown skin wrinkled like tide-rippled sand.

"I've got to have something to do here. I've been meaning to get practising for a while now."

Anaïs stared at her American lover, his head and jaw bandaged, his left leg encased in plaster and hoisted above the bed. She didn't entirely swallow it, but she could not think of a reason not to nip over to La Borie and get his wretched instrument if it made him happy.

"Where is it?" she asked.

"Err, not sure exactly but it's in the loft. Hatch is at the top of the stairs and there's a metal ladder thing that drops down. You can't miss it – should be near the hatch opening since I had it out before Shawcross left. Bring it in its case – be easier."

Anaïs looked long and hard at Starr before determinedly leaving the over-heated hospital room and the lying sod within it.

In 40 minutes, she was back, the awkward trombone case in her hand. Starr smiled appreciatively.

"Never guess who was at the house?" she said as she came in.

"Dacour?"

"Nah, I mean apart from the cops." Starr felt suddenly cold inside the thin hospital blanket. "They searched it, by the way. Had a good rummage before I was allowed to leave with it."

Starr wasn't worried. No-one would have looked inside the bell.

"Who?"

"That funny man who has been fixing your roof. I still don't know his name."

"Monsieur Acrylic Jumper!" Starr felt a rush of relief. "What was he doing at La Borie?"

"Ah, good name. His taste in knitwear is kinda distinctive, you're right. I think it was curiosity mainly. He found you, you know, and thinks he's a bit of a hero. He told me blow-by-blow how he had arrived at the house and heard your shower on but no lights. That raised his suspicions and he had climbed the stairs holding a Roman roof tile in case the intruders were still there." Anaïs imitated the *bricoleur's* exaggerated mime and they both laughed at the spectacle of Monsieur Acrylic Jumper cautiously tip-toeing up the creaky wood stairs to find the bloody and comatose body of Starr in his ransacked bedroom.

"The neurosurgeon said I owed him my life," said Starr between splutters. "And I still haven't paid the man one *sou* for all the work he's done."

"I guess he'll be getting a decent tip."

"*Sans doute!*"

The door opened and the imperious nurse announced that the visitor must leave immediately. Monsieur Starr was to have a CAT scan and the doctors insisted he must have calm.

"I'm just leaving," said Anaïs in a conciliatory voice, soft enough to make a wildcat turn on its back for a tummy-scratch.

The nurse smiled and then her eyes fell on the trombone case propped up on a visitor chair.

"*Qu'est ce que c'est que ça?*"

"Ah," said Starr quickly. "That's just my trombone. I promise only to play it quietly with the mute sock when I'm better."

The nurse and Anaïs exchanged a knowing look, before Anaïs squeezed his hand and sashayed out of the room.

The nurse read out a menu for the next few days and briskly marked his tentative choices before herself leaving him. There was no way he could manoeuvre himself to the trombone to check the labels were still where he had left them but he felt reassured by the presence of the case. He had no doubt whoever had bashed him over the head would be back for them.

The CAT scan was quick. He sat up with his head in a brace to ensure he didn't move while in a room beyond, the neuro team checked for bleeds on a computer screen. Judging by their smiles, he hadn't sprung a leak.

Taking his cue from the light through his hospital blinds it must have been some time in the afternoon when the door to his room opened and Dacour made a furtive appearance. Starr pretended to be asleep but as the inspector settled into a visitor chair, he soon gave up and opened a bleary eye to the grey and crumpled policeman.

"Ah, you are awake, conscious?" Dacour asked superfluously.

"Apparently."

"*Comment ça va?*"

"*Ça va...*" replied Starr. "Before you ask me your questions, there's something I want to ask you," he continued.

The inspector raised an eyebrow and waited.

"The labels. From the Chateau de la Rivière. Did they get taken to the Pessac lab?"

Dacour frowned. "I imagine so. Christine Montreux was leading the whole wine fraud investigation so once the DCF were there the labels were under her command, her jurisdiction. Why do you ask?"

"Is it possible, I mean purely theoretically, that she could have impounded them and not taken them to the Pessac lab?" asked Starr.

"You mean not investigate the forgery? But that makes no sense. She has led the DCF's operation into fake Bordeaux for over three years now. She is a leading authority. She is one of the highest-ranking *Commandants* in the fraud squad. This has been her baby," said Dacour as his face became more and more perturbed. "She had Piezenski into the station and interrogated him for over two hours. I was there when they brought him in. Don't be taken in by her femininity. She's *dure à cuire, vraiment!*"

"A tough cookie. Yeh, I agree with you there. Is it something you could find out? I mean is there any way you could quietly investigate?" Starr persisted.

"Well. I know a few of the *mecs* on the ground here and my nephew works in the Pessac lab, a junior role, but yes, I can probably find out about the wine labels. Why are you so interested?"

"Oh I don't know. Something about Christiane Montreux bothers me. Still bothers me. I'm convinced it was she who sent me that anonymous text message to come to the nursing home and I feel like I've been played by her, you know? Why did she take me into her confidence? Something smells."

"It must be that blow to your head," said Dacour sourly. "Any suggestion that a senior inspector would be, how do you say, *véreux, c'est insupportable!*"

"Look, I'm not making any accusations. I just want to find out about the wine labels, OK?" Starr thought it was time to drop the insinuations that a bent *flic* – literally a maggoty *flic*, as Dacour had called it – could be operating within the pristine ranks of the French police.

"My turn?" asked Dacour. Starr nodded and instantly regretted it. Any movement of his head sent a throbbing pain round his skull like a pinball machine. He grimaced.

"Have you any idea who attacked you in the shower?"

"None at all. I didn't get a look at him and have no idea what anyone would want in my bedroom," Starr replied innocently.

"Tell me again exactly what you remember."

Starr repeated the narrative: the phone calls; the creak on the stair; the black-out. Momentary recovery of consciousness. Black-out again.

"Tell me exactly what you remember seeing in the bedroom," persisted Dacour.

"Drawers out, clothes on the floor, books off bookshelf, bedcovers off, jacket gone," said Starr.

"What was in your jacket?"

"I told you. Just my wallet and my cellphone. And my notebook."

"Notebook?"

"It's an old book of tasting notes but I now use it to remember any odd thing; crossword clues, that kind of thing."

"Anything about Mademoiselle Janneau's murder?"

"Well maybe; just some musings, you know. Questions. Possibilities. Nothing of interest and nothing you and I have not discussed many times over."

"Such as?"

"Well...erm. Such as...Who in the Castillon police department stole Sylvie's cellphone and wiped the text message to de Cazaux? Who planted it in Refeuille's jacket pocket at the Cercle Rive Droite? Who sold the autopsy report to Madame de Cazaux? Who sent me the text about the Maison de Retraite and why? Why has Piezenski not been charged? How did Refeuille die? Was he suicidal or was he pushed? Was he framed or was he really guilty of Sylvie's murder? Why was there absolutely nothing on Sylvie's body of her attacker – not one hair, one thread, nothing. Just musings...you know," Starr's voice trailed off as the throbbing pain in his head started up again.

"You ask a lot of questions, Monsieur Starr. But you are not so forthcoming with answers," said the inspector.

"I don't know what anyone could have wanted," lied Starr. "If I knew I'd tell you. Honestly. By the way, when will Refeuille's autopsy be completed?"

"I am going to the morgue this afternoon, as it happens. The *pathologiste* suggests he was dead before he entered the water." The tired detective's piercing eyes bored into Starr as he delivered the news.

"Murder then?"

"Game not over," replied Dacour with rare humour as he scraped back the plastic chair on the lino floor and left the room.

Starr was asleep when Michel, the solid, the monumental Michel, opened the door and woke him up.

"What's happened?" he blurted out.

"I did not mean to disturb you, Monsieur Starr. The Capitaine has a message for you." He read out from his notebook deliberately. "The wine labels discovered in the cellars of the Chateau de la Rivière. They were not taken to the Pessac laboratoire."

"Ah, OK. *Merci*," said Starr, mind whirring.

The monotony of life in hospital was the best motivation there was to get better. In five days, Starr was sitting up in a chair, his knee no longer suspended in a hoist, his drips and catheter gone. The bandage round his head and jaw had shrunk to a dressing at the back of his head over the shaved patch where he'd had surgery. He could walk a little on crutches, his knee swaying like a dead branch, as far as the bathroom and the coffee machine. He couldn't actually use the coffee machine but it was a destination and he was familiar with its range of options: espresso;

machiato; cappuccino; latte; café crème. Tea came in two flavours only: English Breakfast or Menthe (mint). He was sure they all tasted the same: of plastic.

A uniformed policeman continued to be posted 24/7 outside his room and accompanied him on these short outings. He'd grown fond of Michel in particular and found himself offering girlfriend advice.

La Borie had been locked up after forensics had found no prints. Dacour had not visited since he had relayed the message about the wine labels. Anaïs was his only regular visitor, although Guy de Bachelet had drifted by one afternoon, a half bottle of Bollinger secreted in one overcoat pocket and two flutes in the other. The two men had bent conspiratorially over the cold bubbly wine, like naughty schoolboys. Never had Champagne tasted so good.

Starr had moved the rolled wine labels from his trombone to a pair of socks that was stashed with his few other clothes in a bedside cupboard. There was no obvious way an intruder could enter and steal them but Starr was taking no chances.

He had started having regular physio on his knee and had to try putting weight on the leg. This was the most painful aspect of his recovery, but one he was determined to get through. He was desperate to be home.

CHAPTER

13

"How long before I can drive?" Starr was sitting on the hospital bed, his things packed in a rucksack and his trombone next to him.

The consultant was non-committal but encouraging. *"Bah! Pas longtemps, pas de tout."*

And for once he wasn't lying. Anaïs wheeled the chair, the hospital steel crutches stashed at Starr's side, through the beige and green corridors to freedom, blue skies and the palpable heat of a fine May morning. A nurse would visit him at home three times a week and he was to start sessions in the swimming pool with the monosyllabic Tunisian physio from the hospital.

La Borie was at its best in early summer. Everything was in flower and the vines were lush and sprouting before their first haircut, like curly-headed Victorian boys revelling in unfettered youth. Anaïs parked him at the terrace table and they sat in the sunshine chewing on olives and bread, a bottle of Starr's favourite Billecart-Salmon Champagne cooling in an earthenware jug under the table. "So what was in the trombone?" Anaïs fixed him with her large, warm eyes.

"What do you mean?"

"Oh come on, Franklin. I wasn't born yesterday. You were insistent that I get that thing and I know for a fact you haven't played it more than twice in the six months I've known you."

"You told me yourself the police searched it; nothing there." Starr remained determined to keep Anaïs out of danger.

She took a swig of the cold Champagne and arched a disbelieving eyebrow by way of response. Starr knew she wouldn't press him on this, his first day of freedom but she wouldn't forget it either.

He was so relieved that Le Blond had suggested picking up the labels from the hospital himself. There was no reassuring Michel to keep away Piezenski's heavies now that Starr was home and he was absolutely sure that they'd be back if he didn't get to the forger first.

The Pessac lab had confirmed what he already knew: these were first-rate forgeries carried out with exceptional historic verisimilitude. While there was no way to link them to Piezenski, they were now matched with the photos taken by Dacour at the Chateau de la Rivière's underground tunnel. Christiane Montreux had been arrested in Paris and the creepy Madame Margueron was in custody in Libourne.

Much of this labyrinth had now been exposed, but the core mystery – the minotaur at its centre – that was still unclear. Who had murdered Sylvie if not Refeuille?

Dacour had speculated that perhaps Refeuille had carried out the murders of Sylvie and his mother but then been greedy or attempted to blackmail accomplices like Piezenski and had been murdered as a result. He and Starr had ruminated together sitting in the little smoking kiosk outside the hospital entrance, Starr in a wheelchair and dressing-gown, Dacour in crumpled pleather.

Something wasn't fitting though and Starr continued to feel that Refeuille just wasn't the type to plan and execute a murder in cold blood. He didn't have the steel.

Starr lay with his head in Anaïs' lap as she stroked his head. He looked up at the clear blue sky, the swallows diving high against the sun that warmed the stone table and bench and his broken bones. There were early butterflies on the wisteria and bees hummed on the lavender.

When his cellphone rang, Anaïs grabbed it and refused to give it him.

"Anaïs, please," he pleaded. "It might be important."

"And I'm not?" she arched an eyebrow.

"Nothing is more important than you," he agreed, surreptitiously lunging for the phone.

Missed call. Dacour's number.

Anaïs shrugged her beautiful tanned shoulders and took a long sip of the Champagne as Starr limped on crutches to the top of the garden to get a signal.

"Christiane Montreux has given me a complete statement," Dacour sounded almost peppy. He was breathless and the words stumbled over each other as they raced each other to a distant full stop.

"Paris...arrest...TGV..." the patchy signal reduced Dacour's critical sentence to a staccato piece of runic code.

"Who?" Starr shouted into the phone as it finally went dead.

After several failed attempts to call him back, his frustration knotting his stomach, he limped back to the warm embrace of Anaïs and the cool champagne he loved.

"Dacour knows who did it, but the signal gave up before he could say," he told her languidly.

"Then there's nothing for you to do but stay here and rest," she soothed. "You'll know soon enough."

Getting upstairs was no easy feat and if the prize hadn't been quite as irresistible, Starr might never have made it. Finally he went up backwards on his bottom, dragging his bad leg and powering up on his good.

The sex was urgent, hungry. They tore the clothes from each other, Starr occasionally letting out a yelp of pain as one or other of his sore scars took a hit. But in seconds Anaïs was standing in front of him, the window behind her, half-silhouetted against the sun, her nipples erect, her legs held slightly apart. Desire coursed through his body. Soon they lay trembling and clasping each other long after their heartbeats slowed and their breathing returned to normal.

He kissed her on her lips and she stroked his head and rumpled his hair. And then for no reason, other than perhaps some kind of deep relief, they both burst into laughter, giggling at their mutual lust.

"You sure you'll be OK?" Anaïs was leaving for the private view she couldn't miss.

"What could possibly happen?" Starr replied with irony.

"Don't joke," she said as she started the mini. "I really don't like to think of you here alone."

"Just me and my trombone," Starr said.

"And I do so love your trombone," she said smiling.

He watched the dust settle where the mini had reversed before slowly hopping on his crutches to the stone table where a glass of Champagne still stood undrunk.

Dacour would be in Paris by now and the arrest, presumeably of de Cazaux, planned with the local police squads. He had so wanted to be there at the kill, not admiring his view impotently from 300 miles away.

The promised call didn't arrive for another two hours and when it finally came through, it wasn't the news he craved.

"Starr?" Dacour's monotone voice sounded more than usually tired, as though its owner had lived a thousand years without sleep.

"I'm very sorry but we lost him. By the time we arrived at the office, he had gone. Pouf! Vanished like a ghost. We have roadblocks on the periphérique round Paris, his photo is at both airports and all the border controls. We will find him. It's just a question of time."

"Who, Dacour, who was it? De Cazaux?" But Dacour had hung up and his number went straight to voicemail.

He sat down on the stone steps that cut into a bank at the end of his garden, one gammy leg outstretched, steel crutches at its side.

"Someone has to die," he remembered quoting to Anais just a few months ago in this very spot. And had it made him value life? The sex he'd just had with Anaïs was affirmative, positive, vital, that was for sure. Perhaps the tragic amputation of Sylvie's life had created something in him: a renewed determination to live life, to seize the day.

"Anyone home?" Starr had been too lost in thought to notice the arrival of a sleek Audi 8 outside the house.

Jim Shawcross, one hand bearing a bottle, the other three glasses and a corkscrew, was awkwardly wading across Starr's terrace towards the stone table, sweat stains clearly visible through his crumpled shirt, his hair protruding in wayward tufts from his large burly head. Starr got up to meet him, his inner questioning of the third glass suddenly answered by the appearance of Agnès from the darkened beast of a car that moreorless filled the small driveway of La Borie.

"It's a Gaby specially for you," the bluff Lancastrian pronounced, slapping Starr's back with customary force. "Come on, lad, chin up."

The light was just beginning to turn the azure blue of a May day in the Gironde to a pale shell pink at the horizon. Soon the bee hum would be replaced by the raucous cicadas clattering in the meadows.

"Jim, Agnès, what are you both doing here?" Starr was confused.

"Franklin," Agnès answered gently, putting a hand on his arm. "We are here to thank you. Without you, the Libourne *flics* would never have investigated Sylvie's murder. Everything that has been discovered is down to you. And you nearly gave your life for it." Her deep iris-blue eyes stared straight at Starr, disarming him as always.

The eminent wine buyer poured the ruby wine and the three friends, as they had now indubitably become, raised them in the late spring sunshine.

Starr knew now the murderer was a man and had just escaped arrest in Paris, but he still didn't know his identity. He presumed it was de Cazaux, but something didn't seem to fit.

"Dacour called me to tell me Christiane Montreux had told all. He was leaving to make an arrest in Paris, but," Starr paused to take a gulp of the wine he loved so deeply, "I still don't know who. We got cut off because of the frigging bad signal."

Shawcross smiled conspiratorially at Agnès.

"What, you still don't know?" he said. "Well, while you work it out, I would like to propose a toast."

The three raised their glasses in the early evening light.

"*La verité!*"

AFTERWORD

Valentin Charpentier took a long drag on his cigarette, flipped the butt into the stainless steel communal ashtray designed for the purpose, and slowly went through the revolving door into the stone-flagged lobby inside. His curly grey hair wound round the top of his collar and was unsuccessfully kept in place by the sunglasses that he wore perched, like a tortoiseshell tiara, on his head. The deep tan that was the legacy of his latest exotic holiday, this time the Seychelles, was only just fading.

"Aren't you going to the *en primeur*?" It was the new post-boy, filled with grating enthusiasm.

"I shall probably float by at some stage, *absolument*," Valentin replied vaguely.

"But you have to do your 'top 20'?" persisted ...what was his name?

"Of course. But it is not necessary to taste 200, 250 wines to curate a top 20," Valentin had pressed the vertical arrow for the lift and couldn't wait for it to arrive.

"Oh yeah, because the classification system means you know already what the best ones will be," said the boy knowingly.

The ping of the lift sounded and the doors opened.

"If it were really that simple," said the departing back of Valentin. "They could get you to do it, *non*?" The lift doors closed.

Valentin turned to the mirror and langorously started picking his teeth in front of it with a plastic toothpick he kept in his jacket pocket for the purpose. He was facing the doors and wearing his battle-ready aloof look by the time the lift reached the 5th floor.

He strode past the reception desk, the small warren of editorial partitions where lurked Gilles' sexy little protegée, Sylvie, to his glass office beyond. It had a decent view but nothing to rival that of Gilles' corner suite. Valentin's office was more a storage room than an office. Of course there was a desk, and somewhere a phone and a laptop, but none of those functional clues was visible. Instead what confronted the visitor were towers of books, magazines, newspapers. Every inch of wall had a cutting or chateau leaflet on it and strategically positioned to be impossible not to notice, but so surrounded by clutter that its placing looked accidental, were Valentin's three Roederer Awards for wine writing: three Oscars of the wine journalism world. No-one in history, bar Charpentier, had achieved three annual awards. Nearby was a framed photo of the Saint-Emilion Jurade, all in crimson robes, parading through the medieval streets. If you looked carefully you could just make out the curly hair of the eminent editor among them.

The much-lauded Charpentier really ran *Cuvée*. After all, he would say at exclusive weekend parties at his favourite chateaux, what does Gilles really know about wine, until the bill arrives? It was one of his more successful jokes and never failed to raise a conspiratorial laugh.

Valentin couldn't remember any more the moment when he'd started on the bribery business. What was clear, however, was that it was a great business. He smirked as he listened to Gilles' pronouncements about *Cuvée*; how they should look at a re-design; how he was launching a wine-club; how circulation was a priority. As the smooth little playboy with his trophy wife patronised him with his *Grandes Ecoles* vocabulary and acquired manners, Valentin thought of the bank balance steadily accumulating in his own unmarked Lichtenstein bank account and the hotel enjoying its second season on the slopes of the Atlas Mountains near Marrakech. Other men played golf or fondled little boys. Valentin made money, a lot of money.

Valentin threw the pile of back issues off a large leather swivel chair and sank into it. He would drive down to the Right Bank. It would make collecting much easier and mean he could drive back to Paris whenever he'd had enough. He looked at his watch – almost 18.00h. He'd drop by the steam-room en route home. He felt a bit horny. From a drawer in the invisible desk he pulled a bottle of very decent cognac and poured himself a good glassful. He was letting the rust-coloured liquid open up a bit, as he swirled it around cupping the glass, when he heard Sylvie and Gilles talking in Gilles' office.

He smiled as he caught de Cazaux's oily, flirtatious voice and her earnest enthusiasm. 'No chance,' he thought as he tipped the cognac to catch the light. How clueless was Gilles of what was happening right under his nose. Valentin took a large swig of the warm liquid and let it glow in his mouth before feeling its fire as he swallowed.

"TGV," he heard through the partition wall, followed by Gilles' feeble excuse that he would arrive later. He took a swig and waited to hear Gilles lock his office and silence come in on the tide of a Friday evening. Then he quietly made his way to Sylvie Janneau's cubicle. He turned on her computer, tapped in the password that he'd hacked when she first joined the magazine, and skimmed her emails. There was a hotel booking confirmation in St Emilion, several emails to chateaux accepting or declining invitations to tastings, an email to her mother confirming the dates she'd be away. Valentin took a piece of paper out of her printer and very carefully wrote down the name of the hotel and the TGV arrival time, folding it up and stashing it in an inside pocket of his jacket.

Soon he was outside carried along by the Friday night currents, cigarette in hand, plans forming like origami swans from the folded paper that lay warm in his inside jacket pocket.

II

"Calm down *pour l'amour du ciel*, now slowly," Valentin left the noisy bar of the crowded Plaisance, his BlackBerry held to his ear with his raised shoulder leaving his hands free to open the door. It was a clear night and cold outside on the medieval cobbles of the ancient town. Valentin shivered in his light cashmere jacket. The Illuminated belltower of the Eglise Monolithe rose in deathly splendour against the sky, as a clutch of Ferraris, Maseratis and Range Rovers gleamed darkly in the shadowy parking area at her feet.

"What do you mean, you offered her the Romanée-Conti? Why would you do that? She's a master of wine!"

"Well, keep it in your pants next time, Damien."

"She did what? You saw her text de Cazaux?"

"I can think of a hundred things you could have done, but we are wasting time. Play along – act dumb. Don't let on you had any idea the wine was fake. And don't – on any account – kiss or have sex with her, *comprends*? No DNA. Invite her out tomorrow night for dinner, anywhere in St Emilion, make sure of that."

"Yes of course a restaurant – what else?"

Valentin ended the call and walked slowly to the edge of the cobbled square that was open save for a simple iron handrail to a death-defying drop to the monolithic church below.

The question was not so much how to deal with the fuck-up. Valentin's talents were up to that task, and a plan was already emerging, as his mind performed a series of cognitive moves, turning the consequences like a man solving a Rubik's cube, or a key turning the complex workings of a five lever lock. The question was whether to take the risk or cut loose while he still could. He had long ago planned an exit route, a way to disappear into the thin air of conjecture should it be necessary, but running away smacked of defeat. Valentin was not one to creep into the shadows, to accept he has lost. Valentin was the master of this chess game that we call life.

His mind made up, he tapped in the number.

"Something's up. Can you meet me in the usual place? Good. I'll be there in 20 minutes. Leave the door unlocked."

He pulled up the collar of his cashmere jacket against the biting cold and disappeared into the black shadow of the belltower where his S-class lay in wait.

III

"Oui Hamza, qu'est ce qu'il se passe?" What's up? Valentin stretched a leg to close his office door as the Paris traffic hummed outside.

He lowered his voice and spoke deliberately into his mobile, "De Cazaux? Are you sure?"

"The Orientalist Suite for a week," Valentin repeated committing the details to memory.

"And the name of the second party?"

"Say it is hotel policy – for security – and call me back when you have the name."

Valentin Charpentier looked over the untidy piles of paper that littered every surface of his office – desk, visitor chair, floor, sideboard – to the small window and the smeared view of the city beyond.

He turned the information in his mouth, just as he would a promising wine, letting the full complexities and flavours grow and take shape while he waited for Hamza's call. He didn't have to wait long.

"Ah," he said, swallowing the information whole. "Sylvie Janneau. How very…err..how very… interesting. Oh and Hamza – no discounts."

IV

"Christiane? Oui, Valentin."

"How much do they know?"

"Who is the expert – anyone we know?"

"No. Williams & Williams is too big and too well-connected. I think the best plan is to play along and get as much information as possible. Do we think they'll trace it back to Damien?"

"In that case, we have nothing to worry about. This Monsieur Shawcross will simply leave it to the DCF and you can direct investigations from there."

"When do you arrive in Paris? I can meet you at Charles de Gaulle. Why don't you book us a suite at the Hyatt – usual names? *OK chérie. A vendredi.* I am melting, *comme un glaçon,* just thinking of it!"

Valentin tapped his touchscreen and pushed his tortoiseshell glasses up onto his head where they nestled in the luxuriant head of curls that had enchanted women all his life, from when he was a toddler to this day. He wasn't too concerned about the auction house's discovery. Yes it was a shame that the proceeds of 17 cases of Pétrus hadn't made it to his bank account this time, but there were bound to be a few losses in this game. Shrinkage, you might say.

He'd come across Shawcross before. He was a bumbling Englishman, loved by the chateaux owners because he was a faithful buyer of their wines, but he posed no threat. He wasn't the inquisitive kind. He didn't have the intellect to connect the dots, fortunately.

The wine would go to the Pessac lab and there they'd discover the forged labels, but there was no trail, nothing to link back to the source. A wry smile played on Valentin's lips as he congratulated himself for ensuring that all Refeuille's fraudulent wines were sold in different venues with different provenances. It had taken a while to sign on the various buyers and chateaux, to guarantee an apparently authentic trail, but it had been worth it. His vast collection of auction catalogues and release notes had helped construct credible stories for each and every one of their high-calibre fakes.

What had started as an intellectual game – a challenge, if you like – was now returning almost as much as the bribery business. The costs were higher, but as a diversification that used the same knowledge and many of the same contacts, it had been a very pleasing additional string to his bow.

Valentin slid Berlioz's *Symphonie Fantastique* into his music player and sat back in his reclining Eames chair, his primrose yellow socked feet on its matching leather footstool. The violins combined to develop the 40-bar theme of unrequited love, of passion unreturned. Not that that was any part of Valentin's experience: Christiane was enthusiastic, almost rapacious, in the sack. Valentin liked his music –and his women – full-bodied, symphonic and romantic. He half closed his eyelids to let the music envelop him, drown out the business issues that kept surfacing like unwanted *gonflables,* inflatables, on the smooth waters of his mind.

He would suggest that Christiane transfer to Bordeaux – that way she could keep tabs on any irritating investigations and potentially deflect interest away from sensitive areas. It was a good plan and he'd put it to her when they were in bed, after he'd satisfied her. That would work.

He opened his iPad to finish his column. He was arguing that it was time to reconsider the dominance of the 75cl bottle. After all, why should we continue to bottle wine based on the lung capacity of 17th century glass-blowers? he wrote. Now for the hallmark quotation that always ended the Charpentier personal musings. Valentin flicked through his folder of previous columns to check he hadn't already used the famous Irish toast. No, it was fine. "May your glass be ever full. May the roof over your head be always strong. And may you be in heaven half an hour before the devil knows you're dead," he tapped.

V

Christiane Montreux's head nestled against the tanned shoulder of Valentin Charpentier, her short dark blond hair emphasising her sharp features: her straight nose, her strong jaw, her well-formed large mouth and her round, brown eyes. Her glossy jet black wig lay on the bedside table, an abandoned uniform.

Valentin didn't usually allow her to stay over in his apartment: he preferred the anonymity and control of a hotel. But she deserved a little reward tonight. She'd got the transfer to Bordeaux and from there she would have complete oversight of all DCF investigations into the region. So long as the suicide verdict stuck, they would be home and dry. "Bravo," he thought.

Piezenski's man – the Pole whom he employed solely to forge artists' signatures – had done an exceptional job on the suicide note. Not that he had had any doubts that the studio would rise to the task, but the handwriting was so natural-looking, it had completely fooled the Bordeaux graphologist that the Procureur had insisted check it out. Who would have thought murder was such an easy game?

Press coverage had been about right. A small piece in the *Sud-Ouest* confirming suicide at least ensured word would be out locally that Sylvie Janneau had been found hanged. No-one would fail to understand the message. The arches of the Grandes-Murailles were as public an execution site as the Place de la Concorde in Paris. No-one fucks with Valentin, thought Valentin.

"There is an American who seems interested in the whole case. Not a cop. Not sure who he is," said Christiane lazily, her fingernails playing in Valentin's leonine chest hair.

"Really? What's his name?"

"Monsieur Stall or Starm – I'm not sure. He officially identified the body."

"Interesting. He must have known her then. A father? A relative?"

Christiane wrinkled her nose as if to say 'Who knows?' and moved her lithe body so that she lay on top of her lover, kissing him slowly on the mouth and waiting to feel the familiar response against her thigh.

"Let's not talk about it now," she whispered, brushing her nipples against his and dropping her hand down to grasp him. With one adept move Valentin flipped her onto her back and was soon thrusting deep into her in slow rhythmic movements. He knew exactly how and when to move and could discipline his own desire, waiting for her to tremble and cry out before he let rip to satisfy his own passion. They lay still for some minutes, allowing their breathing to slow, before gently pulling apart. He lit a cigarette.

"You know what they say," he said. "Keep your friends close but your enemies closer. I think you should befriend this American and find out what he's doing, what he wants."

"*Vraiment*? He doesn't appear very important," she said. "He's not involved in wine."

"Exactly. He may have little to lose – that would make him potentially dangerous. Just keep a close eye until the suicide verdict is confirmed by the Procureur and the body released. It should only be a matter of days."

"OK boss. You are the master," Christiane teased him.

"I am. Down on your knees, slave," he said. Christiane climbed out of the bed and knelt on the floor below him. He swung his legs either side of her head and sat up.

"Go on then," he said and dutifully she took him into her mouth.

VI

"Did you get them?"

"What do you mean you couldn't find them? How big is his fucking house?"

Valentin was in his car, driving to a Vinexpo gala at the Musée d'Orsay and the traffic was, as usual, murder. His tuxedo was, if truth be told, slightly tight even without the claret cummerbund that he had unhooked and now lay on the passenger seat next to him. He turned the silver whale of a car through the choked streets, past the lit-up boutiques and delicatessen, the bars and bakeries as the wet, arching cobbles reflected the brake-lights in ruby pools.

"But he said they were in the jacket pocket. Are you sure?"

"*Portable?* Good. What have you got from that?"

"Text from Le Blond – the *graphologiste*?" Valentin made a note to find out why and how this stupid American would know the head of the graphology unit in Marseilles.

"Yes of course I want you to read it out."

'Pessac lab tomorrow morning? You must call and cancel. We need to discover how much they know. Did Starr tell them about the labels and where he got them? Who is it he is seeing?"

"Ah *la belle Hélène.*"

"Yes I know her, but no, she is not on the payroll. Do not attempt a bribe. It is very important that we keep a distance. Say you are a friend of Monsieur Starr and that he is unable to come, but that he will rearrange. If you can, find out all she knows, but don't show your hand. Proceed cautiously. *Compris?*"

Valentin pondered his next move as he made his tortured way towards the Seine. The labels had to be destroyed – it was a new loose end and the only one remaining now that Refeuille's body had been found. The plan he had hatched when Refeuille first called him that ice-cold evening in Saint-Emilion had gone perfectly. It was the Plan B but as a Plan B it was watertight. Frame Refeuille, dispose of the mother and then dispose of Refeuille. He already had a replacement in mind – a young négociant he had met at the Cercle Rive Droite who seemed greedy and ambitious. He had time to groom him.

The difficulty was knowing who this American had confided in. Apart from Le Blond, who presumeably knew at least that he had suspicions, there was the gallery girlfriend, Dacour possibly, and who else?

Valentin tapped his leather steering wheel in frustration. His best strategy, he thought, as clarity came to his mind like settling water, was to replace the labels with genuine contemporary ones. Then the American would be exposed as a fool and they could all move on. To do that they had to be found, and the best time would be while the American was in hospital.

He swung the gleaming car up to the front entrance of the grand old railway station where an official opened his door and invited him to join the throngs on the red carpet. Valentin flashed a set of perfect, even teeth as a hundred flashbulbs turned to capture the famous wine editor, grabbed his dinner jacket and with one continuous move threw it nonchalantly over his shoulder while tossing the car keys to the parking boy, his tortoiseshell glasses nestled in the cloud of curls that adorned his cherubic face.

"Showtime!" he thought.

VII

Before driving down to the river and along its banks to Chateau de la Rivière, Valentin took the road that led east along the Saint-Emilion escarpment. He had to be quiet, even though the Chateau's bins were stored a distance from the house and the chai. He let the purring engine idle as he slid out of the driver's seat and flipped open one after another of the green Castillon wheelie bins. Sure enough, there were the white disposable overalls that he had seen the day before. Termites! How de Bachelet had cursed at their discovery. And who would have thought they'd be so useful? He bundled up two of the papery suits and two masks and stashed them under the carpet of his boot. Quietly he urged the lid shut, gently closed the driver's door and slowly turned the big

German car, like a silver shark swimming in the dark, down towards the sleeping Dordogne and along the D670 westwards.

A full moon was rising and hung suspended over the dark vineyards, lighting up a little stone pigeonnier here, a tobacco barn there, and casting long impenetrable shadows into the half-light.

Piezenski and his handwriting forger were already in the cellar room when he arrived. He squeezed his considerable frame, swollen with good living, down through the hatch door and round the winding stone steps to the tunnel. Light and the murmur of bass Russian voices seeped out from the little cellar room.

"*Merci*," said Valentin simply and then quickly gave the instructions for the suicide note. It must be written on Petit Girondin paper. He handed the Pole a page of Sylvie's handwritten tasting notes that he had stolen from her desk some weeks before. He routinely plundered her nuanced notes for his own articles – it saved time and she never suspected.

"Signature?" asked the Pole.

"*Ah non!* I do not have a copy of her signature. She signs herself 'Sylvie Janneau' that I can tell you, but I do not have a sample."

"*Tant pis.* But the cops are unlikely to check so long as the handwriting is correct."

The three men all nodded. Valentin confirmed he would drop by the atelier in Bordeaux the following afternoon and handed over a roll of 100 €50 notes.

Before the clock on the tower of the Eglise Monolithe had struck midnight, Charpentier was in the hotel bar, enjoying a restorative cognac with a group of well-oiled negociants. He was soon buying them a round and agreeing to meet for dinner on the next day.

An alibi was not strictly necessary, since he was sure that the suicide staging would convince the Castillon '*poulets*' but he was a careful man, whose meticulous attention to detail had served him well.

He would leave the party at 11pm precisely on the pretext of fetching some interesting catalogue from his car. That would give him time to meet Refeuille and Sylvie, Refeuille having dropped in the rohypnol to her wine as he was adept at doing with his many sexual conquests. They would walk to the Grandes Murailles. He would park his car right next to the arches making it easy to put on the overalls and the mask. Once they were there he would tell Refeuille to scarper. She wouldn't even recognise him and with the knots that he had been practising in place, one kick of the wine crates and that would be that. The blue nylon rope would do the rest. He blew an imaginary candle out. Gone. He'd then plant the suicide note in her handbag, replace the overalls under the car's carpet, move the car to its parking space at the Hostellerie de Plaisance and saunter along to the restaurant with the catalogue. A generous bottle of Armagnac would soon dull the memories of the already lubricated négociants and *voilà!* Problem solved. Later that day he'd put the overalls in a black bin liner and dump them in one of the municipal recycling lay-bys.

If, for any reason, the police suspected murder, Refeuille was well framed and would take the hit.

The great Valentin scrubbed his teeth and got into his favourite dark blue silk pyjamas. He would sleep like a baby tonight.

VIII

"What made him change the verdict?" Valentin had celebrated his own genius a little prematurely. An acute observer would have noted a tic on his left temple showing his irritation, but Valentin was alone and unobserved.

"The American? Then get close to him. Confide in him. Pretend you suspect Dacour of being sloppy, he'll like that."

Valentin launched Plan B like a general deploying a second army from his safe war-room many kilometres from the front.

"Yes you must plant the mobile on Refeuille and find a way of discovering it – that way you can arrest him. The Right Bank En Primeur is perfect. See if you can go with the American; that would be ideal. Of course delete Refeuille's texts – he needs to look guilty, *ma chérie.*"

Valentin hadn't yet confided in Christiane the essential part of his Plan B that really depended on her full co-operation. He knew he had to wait his moment and ensure that a combination of devotion to him and personal gain for her would win the day. Even he, the master manipulator, was just a little anxious, however, that matricide might be a step too far even for the ruthlessly ambitious Montreux.

He was at home enjoying a fine Montrachet *grand cru* to the swelling fourth movement of Mahler's Fifth, when he made the call.

"*Chérie*, you know how I hate being apart from you, how I long for the moment when we can be together completely, as one." He waited for the breathy response he had hoped for.

"If I could, I would be in Saint-Emilion tying these few loose ends," he crept slowly towards his prey.

"In fact I hate that you are there having to finalise our business," he lied.

No remonstrations were a good sign.

"But I think you will find it easier because there has been no contact for so many years, decades even," he continued.

"Yes, *chérie*, your mama. She has had her life. She is frail and unhappy. In many ways it will be a gift – a release." He paused anxiously in case there was an objection from the other end of the line.

"*Non, non*, nothing violent of course. Just a soft pillow over her head. She will feel nothing. Just drift into sleep, really. You must just wait for all physical struggle to cease. It will appear that her heart gave out. No suspicions."

"Remember to enter the room from the garden – no-one must see you until the alarm is called and you can be on the investigating team. Ah *ma chérie*, how I long to kiss your breasts, to lick you in those secret places you love and breathe you in. I can taste you now in my imagination. You are my soulmate, my desire." The tender love song of Mahler's *Adagietto* created the perfect backdrop to his phone sex. He needed her fully committed. "Yes, I am licking you, sucking you, oh and now my fingers are exploring you, deep inside, my mouth is all over you. I want you, now," On he went satisfied by the sighs and heavy breaths he could year from his lover in her hotel room in Libourne.

He paused before adding, "Call the American and get him over. We need him on a short leash, always close. That way you will know if he is putting two and two together." He laughed. "As if! He is American after all!" he hung up still laughing under his breath.

IX

"I had no idea you were coming down," said Refeuille, "Or I'd have organized a dinner for you. Something celebratory. I have to stay out of sight – Dacour and his *poulets* are still after me you know."

Valentin smiled paternally at his greedy *protegé*.

"No problem," he said. "I'm happy to see you incognito. The beard really suits you by the way," he smirked.

Valentin wasn't used to eating at what was effectively a transport café. The queues of long-distance trucks were parked nose to tail all along the roadside either side of the modest little brasserie in one of those villages spliced into two by the main road from Bordeaux to Bergerac. But the house red was remarkably quaffable and in the midst of perhaps 70 other men, they were as anonymous as it was possible to be, both in jeans and T-shirts, Valentin having removed his gold Rolex and slipped it into the glove compartment of the Merc earlier.

Valentin needed Refeuille to go to the *toilettes* and was refilling his water tumbler assiduously to achieve that end.

About half an hour in, he was duly rewarded. He slipped the rohypnol into Refeuille's glass of wine and waited for the fizzing to subside.

Refeuille was already a little drunk and before they could order a nice *île flottante* or a coffee *glace*, Valentin winked at the waitress, paid and told her he was going to get his companion off to bed in his sleeper pod. "He's driven from Zaragossa," he confided to her. "Exhausted!"

Valentin bundled him into the back of the Merc and sped off west towards the coast. He hadn't long to catch the height of the outgoing tide and anyway wanted to get back to Paris that night. The least time he spent in Saint-Emilion the better.

It was remarkably easy to hit Refeuille hard over the head with the car jack. He watched carefully for any signs of life then pushed his limp body into the Garonne off the small bridge. There was a muted splash but no-one but the ghosts of the Knight Templar would have heard it.

Wiping the jack carefully with the toilet roll and wet wipes he'd packed, he dumped the bloody paper into the river after the body, carefully stowed the car jack back into its moulded case and swung the shark of a car back toward the north and the motorway that would get him to Paris before dawn.

X

The oily De Cazaux called him into his office with ill-concealed delight. It was not long after lunch and there was a quiet afternoon siesta vibe at this time. De Cazaux's desk was immaculate as always. A bronze Ormulu inkwell spoke to his acquired elevated social status while the silver framed photo of his twin boys in matching sailor suits communicated biological status. The De Cazaux genes would live on.

"Valentin," he said seriously, rubbing his eyes with their long, thick eyelashes. "I'm sorry about this."

With that two uniformed officers stepped out from behind the large office door and took an arm each of the famous wine editor.

"What is this about?" Valentin struggled to slow the rapid beating of his heart in his ribs.

"We would like you to come to the station to answer some questions, that's all," said the older of the two, robotically.

"Am I being arrested?"

"No, not at this time. Our colleagues in the Libourne police are on their way and it has to do with their investigation."

"Ah I see," lied Valentin who did not see at all. Christiane must have ratted him out. How could she? He'd make her pay, but that was for another day, a different story. At least he wasn't being arrested. There was a chance he could talk himself out of it...but why take the risk? Better to slip away before that ill-looking detective reached the capital.

"May I just collect my coat from my office and quickly visit the bathroom?"

The policemen shrugged at each other.

As he returned to his dark den, filled with auction catalogues and past editions of *Cuvée*, a sudden break in the cloud allowed a shard of light to slant through the small window and catch the photo of the Jurade with the great wine writer just visible in his crimson robes. His eyes drank in the tools of his trade for a final time before he picked up his cashmere coat from the hook on the back of the door and turned his back on the office, his job as deputy editor and so much more.

As he turned into the corridor, he glanced down five storeys to the revolving door and pavement below. Three police cars were parked along the street and he counted four uniformed officers guarding the entrance. "*Putain!*" he swore under his breath and snapped the plastic toothpick in two in his jacket pocket.

There was one final card to play.

Claudine, the office receptionist, was knocking on 60, her deep dyed maroon hair fooling no-one. She had been the butt of many of Valentin's sexist jokes with the office lads. He had never seen a reason to be civil to her, and was slightly regretting that omission now. He had a few precious minutes to turn on the charm but confidence was never something he was short of.

He smiled meaningfully at her and asked her for the keys to Monsieur de Cazaux's bathroom.

She raised an eyebrown in enquiry. "You know, on the fourth floor," Valentin's eyes searched hers as deeply as he dare.

"*Ah bien sûr, Monsieur,*" she was busy retrieving a small key from one of the drawers in her desk.

Valentin smiled reassuringly at the two uniforms and left the offices of *Cuvée* for the stairs. The door to what had been De Cazaux's private bathroom opened into a small lobby. Valentin quickly locked the door behind him leaving the policemen waiting on the outside. All that remained of the old fixtures was the large porcelain basin with its ornate taps. Several years ago, builders had ripped out the bathroom to create a small store accessed by the service lift whose beaten metal doors were to Valentin like the pearly gates themselves. He stabbed impatiently at the plastic button to call the lift, while turning on both taps to mask the noise.

By the time the cops realised that the water they could hear on the inside of the door had been running far too long, Valentin had escaped into the underground carpark beneath the building and was edging the silver S-Class through the barrier at the rear.

He set the GPS for a tiny village high in the Pyrenees astride the invisible Spanish border. There he had long owned a modest house, shuttered against the vicious winters and deep snows. The couple who looked after it for him had never met him. They didn't even know his name. He was a generous, mysteriously absent patron who sent gifts every Christmas and paid them handsomely direct from an unnamed bank account registered in Lichtenstein.

Valentin screeched through Paris, not so fast as to attract attention but fast enough to leave the City of Light behind him before the *poulets* and that crumpled detective from Libourne would realise the truth. Once he was on the A10, he urged the smooth S-Class onto its top cruising speed, fumbling in the glove compartment for a cheap little mobile phone he would use for calls with Refeuille, replacing the disposable sim cards each time.

The house would be opened up, the heating put on and the fridge filled with some immediate essentials. The couple were excited at last to be readying the house for its absent owner. They opened the shutters; cut flowers from the garden; put fresh linen on the big double bed and a hearty *cassoulet* ready to heat up. The stage was set; Valentin – or Georges Verlon as he now would be – closed one chapter of his eventful life and opened another.

Printed in Great Britain
by Amazon